YOUR CRAZY LIFE

A revealing novel about the secrets of life and death
and why we keep coming back

KEITH CASARONA

Cover and book design:
Naomi C. Rose www.ncrdesigns.com

Text set in Cambria

ISBN: 978-1987596281

Bartels Publishing
Sedona, Arizona

Dedication

My Cast of Characters

Joe   Mary   Roy   Mabel   Charlie   Rose
Bob   Fanny   Norma   Ed   Fay   Elizabeth
Marty   Mike   Debbie   Elaine   Ben
Roy B.   Gary   Tom   James P.
James O.   Jack   Hedy
Gregory   Devicka
Cecilia   Jessie
Kaisan   Kelly
Sherilyn

Thank you all for being my teachers!

Prologue

Reality is merely an illusion,
albeit a very persistent one.
– Albert Einstein

Maybe the secrets of life and death are a lot simpler than we could ever imagine.

Maybe, just maybe, one of the wisest men to live in our times told us the secret in just one sentence.

What if Albert was right?

What if your life is an illusion? What if your life was no more real than a movie made in Hollywood?

What if you are the writer, director, and main character in the craziest story ever told— the story of your life!

If that is true, then maybe believing your story is real could be the only true hell there is.

But really, could your story be any more real than the story to follow?

Everyone loves a good story.

This is Mary's story. Mary's and Michael's, Kristin's and Eric's, Kort's and Leni's. And perhaps, in one way or another, it's everyone's story.

The screenplay is written.

The actors are cast.

The director is ready.

Lights, camera, action!

Chapter 1

What a Fool I Was

1971. Munich. Mary sits in a wheelchair facing a window. On the table next to her is an empty bottle of sleeping pills. A teardrop falls on the photograph she holds in her wrinkled hand. The photograph is of her son Michael and his fiancée Kristin Nevaeh before the war. They are standing together and smiling. Mary's hand goes limp and the photograph falls to the floor.

1943. Dachau Death Camp. Men in prison clothes pull Kristin's naked body from a cart of other dead women. They toss her body into a small carriage and shovel it into a blazing crematorium oven.

1944. France. An American soldier walks on a deserted road. He pulls a photo from his pocket of Mary and a young girl. After taking a quick look, he shakes his head, and shoves the photo back into his pocket.

Date unknown. Location unknown. A hand presses the final prick of a tattoo needle into the inside of a forearm. The design of a rose winding around a dagger in the shape of a large letter E is now complete.

1971. Munich. In the late afternoon, a wooden coffin sits on the ground next to an open grave at the Ostriedhof Cemetery. Lying on the coffin's lid are ten yellow roses. The gravestone reads "Mary Johanson 1897-1971."

A short distance from the grave stands a stone statue of a young angel. She holds a rose in one hand. The other hand points skyward. Following the angel's pointed finger, we move through thickening clouds, past the bounds of our small planet, through the blackness of outer space, and into a 1930s movie theater.

Warm light pulsates from vintage lighting throughout the theater's majestic lobby. Rich maroon carpets cover the floor, and walnut panels line the walls. Instead of a ceiling, there is only sky—a view into the universe of planets and suns, swirling galaxies.

Kristin Nevaeh, a beautiful young woman in a long white flowing dress, moves swiftly through the lobby doors and into a lower auditorium. She has pale skin and shiny black hair. Just as she steps onto a spiral staircase, a middle-aged man appears instantly before her. It is Eric Johanson. Eric is tall, and wears a German World War I uniform. "Kristin," he says, grabbing her arm. "He's not going to back out again, is he?"

"No, Eric." Kristin wrestles her arm free. "He won't. Trust me."

"But he's up there. In the auditorium. Watching the whole bloody mess again."

"He'll be fine," says Kristin in a soothing voice. "I promise."

A black cat patters over, and Kristin kneels down to pet it. "I hope you're right," says Eric. "Michael is one of the key players. We need him to make the story work."

"I know. I know. I'll talk to him."

"The timing is perfect. You know Michael must be the first to go."

Kristin turns to Eric. "I know. Trust me. He'll go." She heads up the staircase.

Eric shakes his head, and he vanishes with the cat.

Dramatic music and voices echo from above as Kristin climbs the stairs. At the top of the landing she faces two massive golden doors to the main auditorium. With a sigh, she opens one of the doors and walks in.

The main auditorium is as majestic as the lobby. Gold panels and colorful gemstones surround an enormous screen. The music of Richard Wagner's Liebestod rings through the air. Kristin stands at the top of the balcony area and peers down the rows of seats. There in the middle of a row, half way down from the top, a young man slouches in his seat. It's Michael Johanson. He sits there alone.

Kristin can see Michael is very distressed. His shoulders are hunched, and he pulls on his eyebrow as he watches the scenes on the screen.

Michael and Kristin are making love. Michael declares his undying love for her.

Michael waves his hand and the scene changes.

Michael as a young boy is sitting on his father's lap. Both Eric and Michael are laughing.

Michael waves his hand again.

Kristin and Michael are kissing in a park. Kristin lets one yellow rose drop out of her hand to the ground.

Michael wipes a tear from his eyes. Kristin at the top of the balcony wipes away tears too. Michael waves his hand again.

Michael with a knife in his hand is screaming and threatening his father, Eric.

Michael shakes his head and waves his hand again.

Kristin walks down the aisle to Michael and puts her arms around his shoulders. "Oh my God, Michael, I can't believe you're watching all this again." She waves her hand. The music stops.

"The more I watch what happened down there last time," says Michael, "the more I think we're crazy to go back."

"What? And miss all the fun? I'm going back. We all are. We need you, Michael. The whole thing just wouldn't be as good without you. The timing is perfect."

Michael waves his hand at the screen and the flashing scenes stop. "I can't go through this again."

"Please, Michael, I know you can do it this time. You can't back out now. We're all counting on you. *I'm* counting on you."

Michael gazes into Kristin's eyes and sighs. "I know. But couldn't we at least tone it down a bit?"

Kristin laughs. "Tone it down?"

"Hey, I'm the first one to admit it. I bit off way more than I could chew. We made the story way too tough last time."

"Lets face it. We all thought it was a good plan. Otherwise we would've never tried it in the first place."

Kristin waves her hand. They are instantly transported out of the auditorium and into a beautiful rose garden full of yellow roses. Kristin touches one of the roses. It breaks apart and the petals fall into her palm. She shakes her head at the broken flower.

"You see, Michael," says Kristin, "it could have turned out very differently. You had a real opportunity to forgive Eric and the others. But you went to war—the one thing you hate the most. That story is over now. We've all learned from it. Now it's time to prove we can be different. Come on, Michael, one more time?"

Michael touches a rose. It too crumbles in his hand. "How many times have I fallen into the trap of patriotism? How many wars has it been? How many people have I killed, just because some government, some church, some politician said so? Me and my strange idea of loyalty. And this last time with the Nazis and World War II...my God, what a fool I was."

As Michael speaks, he morphs back into himself as a German World War II soldier.

Chapter 2

God What Have You Done to Us

Michael trudges with his friend, Johan Voss, through the decimated city of Nancy, France on September 17, 1944. Both grip machine guns at their sides. Both have smears of dirt and blood over their faces. Both are exhausted—they've been in combat for seven days straight. Rain trickles down and lightning strikes in the distance. They approach a house that took a direct mortar hit to the roof. It was clearly once a beautiful home.

After Michael kicks the door open, he and Johan step inside. In the dim light, Michael notices a pile of debris in the middle of the floor. Lying dead in the pile is a young French woman. Her dress is yellow with little flowers on it, and her long blond hair covers her face. A large wooden beam from the roof lies across her hips. When Michael reaches over to brush her hair from her eyes, he discovers yet another dead body under the woman—a small girl about four years old. Michael turns away in disgust and leaves the house. Johan follows him.

The sky is filled with dark clouds and smoke from burning buildings. Michael stares at his machine gun as if he's seeing it for the first time, for what it is—an instrument of death. "What I'm I doing?" he asks himself. "I'm helping to create this living hell!" He throws his weapon into the mud, drops to his knees, and lets out a primeval scream. "God, where are you?" He raises his arms with clenched fists. "God, what have you done to us? Either you care nothing for us or are a fool. Either way, I curse you!"

Lightning flashes. "You'll get us detected," yells Johan. He grabs Michael and the gun then pushes Michael towards the door of another half-destroyed house.

Johan gets Michael inside the house and makes him sit down on some rubble. Then he puts Michael's gun down. Keeping his eyes on Michael, he gets out a cigarette, lights it up, and offers it to Michael. But Michael shakes his head no.

"What're you doing?" asks Johan, taking a drag of the cigarette. "Trying to get us both killed? What is it? The woman back there? We've seen dead people before."

"The woman? Yes, it's the dead woman. It's all the dead women and children. It's my dead sister and your dead father. It's all the dead people. It's the death we are spreading on this goddamn manure pile of a war."

Michael takes out a letter from his pocket and waves it at Johan. "This is a letter from my father. I haven't talked to him in four years. The bastard still writes to me." Michael reads from the letter. "'I'm proud of you, Michael. You are doing your duty to your country, our beloved Fatherland.'"

Michael waves the letter at Johan again. "Can you believe it? He's very proud that I'm now in the killing business. Yes, he's very happy. Now that I'm killing his enemies. The people who had the misfortune to be born on the other side of some boundary line. The people who speak a different language than us. The people who don't believe the same things we do, or in the same god that I use to believe in."

"We kill because we've been trained to kill," says Johan, "because we have orders to kill. Did we really have a choice to do otherwise?"

Michael sighs. "Of course we had a choice. Every person does. I made the wrong choice." His back straightens. "It's time to stop all this insanity. It's time to surrender."

Johan rubs his cigarette into the floor with his boot. "Surrender? Two months ago, a few men tried to surrender to the Americans. They were shot. The Americans laughed afterwards, claiming they didn't know the German words for surrender. I saw it all."

"Then we should stand up to our people and say 'no more,'" said Michael. "That's really the choice I should have made in the beginning of the war. Jail would have been better than this."

"Are you crazy? They'd put us up against a wall and shoot us."

"So there's no way out of this hell?"

"We all got caught in its web. No one saw this war coming."

"My Kristin knew."

"She did?" asks Johan.

Michael swallows hard. "She tried to tell me. But I refused to listen. If only I had..." He gazes at the dark clouds through a large hole in the roof, remembering another time, before the war began.

Chapter 3

Kristin Knew What Was Coming

Michael and Kristin walk in the park next to Ostriedhof Cemetery in Munich. It's a late afternoon in early September 1938. Kristin has one yellow rose in her hand. Her arms are crossed, and she's frowning. Michael spins her around and kisses her. They look into each other's eyes.

"We really need to talk," says Kristin. Her words spill out fast. "I know you hate it every time I bring it up, but it's time we made a decision—before it's too late. I know you don't believe it. But my father is sure we're all heading towards war. I do too. He says we need to leave Germany now, before something bad happens to all of us."

Michael lets go of Kristin. "Not this again."

"I have a bad feeling about what's happening around us," says Kristin. "Can't you see it? We need to leave this place. And since my father won't go without me and I won't go without you, it all comes down to you, Michael. This could be the most important decision of our lives."

"What will I do for work? What about my job here?"

"My aunt in America will put the three of us up until we can get on our feet. And since we both speak some English—"

"No, Kristin! I'm not leaving Germany. This is where I was born. This is my home. This is all I know. My family is here. The people I love are here."

Kristin takes a step away from Michael. "The people that hate the Jews are here too."

Michael hesitates for a moment. "You know the law. You just have a small percentage of Jewish blood. It won't be a problem. You're only one quarter Jewish and the Mischlinge law states that if you marry a non-Jew you'll be fine. Do you think that Hitler is going to ship everyone with even a little bit of Jewish blood in them out of Germany?"

"If not him, others would have no problem doing so," says Kristin.

"There's no way it will ever happen," says Michael. "Look how Hitler brought this country out of the depression, in just a few years. Germany is now one of the strongest countries in the world. Hitler doesn't want war. No sane man wants war. Not after the carnage of the last one. I'm sure he's a man of peace. You must believe me."

"Believe you? Are you willing to trust your future, my future, and my father's to some man— some politician?"

"I really believe he only wants what is best for us. Just like I do."

"Michael, I have a really bad feeling. Some of my friends have already been shipped out for relocation. How can you be so sure my father and I won't be next?"

"Listen to me. My uncle is the deputy police chief of Munich. He'd tell me if something like that were going to happen. You must believe me. I would never let anything happen to you or your father. I'd die first. I've never been more sure about anything in my whole life."

Michael reaches up and brushes the hair out of Kristin's eyes. She gives Michael a slight smile.

"So it's settled," Michael announces.

"I guess I have no choice but to trust you again." Kristin gives Michael a kiss. "So when are you going to tell your family about us getting married?"

"I'll tell everyone when I get back from Berlin next month. My job is going very well there. I'll walk you home. By the way, what do you think of a garden wedding?"

They gaze into each other eyes and kiss again. Kristin lets her rose fall to the ground. She takes Michael's arm, and they start walking out of the park. "Lets take the long way home," she purrs.

Chapter 4

What a Strange Question

Michael hops out of a car on a busy street in the older part of Munich. After retrieving his suitcase from the backseat, he turns to a young man behind the steering wheel. "Thanks for the ride, Robert. I'm going to walk the rest of the way. I need to get a bottle of wine. Tonight I'm going to tell my family about my marriage to Kristin."

"Well, good luck. I wish you and Kristin the very best."

"Thanks."

Happy to be back after a month away, Michael strolls down the street. The eight hundred-year-old city is radiant—the sights, the colors, the smells of fresh baking bread at the nearby bakery. Friends wave hello from across the street, and Michael waves back with a big smile. He's euphoric. The stars are in alignment. He's twenty-one years old, young and healthy. He has a great job. He's in love and engaged to the prettiest woman in the city— at least he thinks she is. Could things be anymore perfect?

When Michael reaches the wine shop, he finds the door and windows boarded up. The word "Juden" is crudely painted everywhere. Michael tries to see through a slit in the boards. But it's too dark inside. "These people were my friends," he mumbles. "What's happened to them?" There's no one else on the street now. No one there to answer.

Michael hurries towards home, pushing away any thoughts about the wine shop. This is his big day, when his family will know that he and Kristin are engaged. He won't let anything ruin that.

As he gets closer to his house, music floats from the open kitchen window. It's Richard Wagner's Liebestod playing on the radio. On the window's ledge is the family's cat, Elisa. Michael pets her black fur. "You're the best friend this family has because you love us all no matter what."

Elisa purrs in response.

Michael looks into the kitchen. Sunlight filters through the window, and there is flour dust in the air. Michael's mother, Mary, is there, kneading bread dough. She is now a plain woman. But Michael knows she was a real beauty in her day. As he watches her, he can't help but notice the sadness that hangs around her like a heavy cloak, the sadness that's always been there.

Michael steps through the door, and a warm feeling fills him. He's home again. His great-grandfather built this house one hundred and twenty years ago with old world craftsmanship throughout. The German attention to detail was everywhere.

"Michael? Is it you?" Mary shouts.

Michael sets his suitcase down and hangs up his coat. Mary stops kneading and looks up at her son as he walks into the kitchen.

"It's me. I'm home. Sure smells good in here. Did you miss me?"

"Of course I did. I cooked all day for you. How was Berlin?"

"It went very well. I think we'll get the contact. If we get it, I'm buying you a pretty new dress."

"A pretty dress. That's nice." Mary's words come out flat. She begins kneading the dough again, but her eyes glaze over like she's lost in some distant moment.

Michael steps closer and speaks softly. "Mother, why aren't you happy?"

She abruptly walks to the sink, keeping her back to Michael. "What do you mean?"

"I mean are you happy?" asks Michael. "With the way your life has gone?"

"What a strange question." Mary turns off the radio and washes her hands. Elisa, the cat, jumps through the open window and onto the kitchen counter. Mary absently pets her as she answers. "I'm as happy as any woman could be. I have two wonderful children and a man that takes care of me. What more could a woman want?"

Elisa leaps to the floor and out of the kitchen.

Michael knows his mother speaks half-truths. He walks over and gives her a hug from behind. Mary's face gets red and her shoulders tense. She's not use to any kind of physical attention. "What are you doing now, you silly boy?"

"I'm giving my mother a hug!"

Suddenly Michael's sixteen-year-old sister, Leni, appears in the kitchen doorway. She looks like a tomboy with her short blond hair and in the pants she always wears. Tears stain her cheeks. "I hate being a girl. I wish I were a boy!" she cries.

"Why would you say such a thing?" asks Mary.

Leni swipes tears away with the back of her hand. "Father hates me! He hates me because I was born a girl and not a boy like Michael."

"That's not true," says Mary. Her eyes urge Michael to say something. But he stays silent.

Leni turns away and slumps up the staircase to her room.

"What's with you kids today?" says Mary.

"Nothing's up with us," says Michael. "Leni is right. I've seen the mean ways Father treats her. He's downright cruel at times. I have tried to pretend it isn't so but I can't any longer. Just tell me why he does it."

Mary's lips form a tight line. She shoves her fists into the dough, kneading faster.

Michael shakes his head and walks out the back door and into the yard.

Chapter 5

The Rotten Apple

Michael's father, Eric Johanson, is pruning an apple tree in the yard. He's in his early fifties. He has always been a hard man, and the years have clearly been hard on him. Deep lines run across his forehead and down his cheeks, his razor-cut hair and mustache are gray, and he moves with a slight limp from a war wound. Eric doesn't notice Michael as he walks up behind him.

"Father, why do you treat Leni so badly?" Michael's mouth feels dry—he's never confronted his father before.

Eric spins around. "You're home and this is how you greet your father?"

"Leni is crying, Father. Why are you so cruel to her?"

"I treat Leni the way she needs to be treated."

"But you've always treated her differently than me."

"Of course, I have. She's a girl and you are a boy."

"What does that mean?"

"It means a new order is coming and with it, a new Germany! The German woman of the future must be every bit as strong as the German man. All German men and women must be willing to fight for our freedom. Our enemies made us eat dirt after the war. No one will ever do that to me—to us—ever again. So what I do to Leni, I do for Leni's sake."

"You want women to be as hard as men?"

"The new German must be willing to do whatever our country asks. The time for weak and stupid women like Leni and your mother is over."

"How can you say such things about your wife and daughter?"

"Michael, you are a foolish boy. You must know war is coming. The end of the last world war was just the beginning. It's time for us to take back what belongs to us. It's time to make them all pay with their blood!"

Michael lets out a long breath. When had his father become such an angry bitter old man? Or had he always been that way? "Father, no one wants war."

"I expect you and your sister to do your duty when the time comes," says Eric, pointing a thick finger at Michael. "For our country, our Fatherland."

"Even if that means killing?"

"Absolutely."

"Have *you* ever killed anyone?"

Eric lifts his chin with pride. "Yes. I've killed for my country. I had no choice—it was him or me. In France. 1917."

A faraway look comes over Eric's face.

Eric is running fast. Artillery shells explode in the distance. He leaps into a shell creator, startling a young French soldier, Frank Costello. The Frenchman hesitates. Eric shoots his rifle, hitting Frank in the stomach. Frank drops his gun and puts his hands up. His eyebrows weave together, like he can't understand how this could happen. Eric takes his rifle with his bayonet and drives it into Frank's chest.

Eric grins at the memory as he looks up at Michael. "Very soon, you will be asked to do your duty. What will you do, when that time comes? Will you be a coward? Or answer the call to Germany?"

"I don't want to kill or die for anyone," Michael says. "I've seen what the war has done to you and others and I want no part of it. I want to get married and have children. I want to have your grandchildren—Kristin's and my children."

"What?" Eric's eyes widen. "Who'd you say?"

"Kristin. I'm marrying Kristin Nevaeh."

"That Jewish bitch? Over my dead body!"

"What're you talking about?" asks Michael. "She's only one quarter Jewish."

"I don't want grandchildren from that Jewish whore!" Eric shoves his face into Michael's. "Who cares if they'd only be one fourth Jewish? That's plenty enough to soil our family's blood. I'd look at your children, but see only their little Jewish rat eyes."

Michael backs away. He's never heard his father talk this way. "How can you say such things?"

"Do you see this rotten apple?" asks Eric, picking a rotten apple off the ground. "This rot started from just a tiny bit of rot. The Bible says, 'A little leaven ferments the whole lump!' I can't believe you would do this to me, our family, and to God!" Eric throws the apple at Michael's feet.

"To God?" says Michael. "I saw the belt buckle on your uniform from the war. Do you remember what it said on it?"

"Of course. Gott Mit Uns. God is on our side."

"Right," says Michael. "And was God on Germany's side in the war? On your side, Father? Because you lost, remember?"

"Uh..."

"You want to talk about rot?" yells Michael. "Rot is people thinking that God is only on their side. That is the only true rot in this world. Parents sending their children to war to die and to kill for their rotten misguided thinking. Rot is their children's dead bodies rotting in the ground for their belief systems." Michael picks up the rotten apple on the ground and hurls it back at Eric, hitting him in the shin. Then he storms back into the house.

In the kitchen, Mary cautiously lifts her eyes to Michael. "Supper will be ready soon," she announces in a forced cheerful voice.

"I'm not eating here today," says Michael. "Father has said too much to me. And you, on the other hand, have said nothing at all. I know you're holding something back from me. I hope it's worth it."

Mary squeezes her eyes shut, and says nothing.

Michael slams the front door behind him as he leaves.

Chapter 6

The Best Kind of Love There Is

Rain falls as Michael storms away from his house. It's the same street he's walked down a thousands times before. But like so many things today, it looks different, the people look different, everything is different. Michael returns to the boarded up Jewish wine shop. People show no concern as they bustle around him. He stops for a moment and stares at the window. The painted insult drips down the window from the rain.

"When did this happen?" he asks himself. "When did Germany change? Why didn't I see it? Why didn't I see that Hitler is just the mouthpiece for people like my father? The beaten veterans from the last world war. The men who want another war. A war for their God, their country, but most of all for their foolish pride. Kristin was right all along. We need to leave Germany as soon as possible—before it's too late."

Michael walks through the heavy doors of Burgerbraukeller Beer Hall. A sign says, "At this location, the National Socialist Party was born." This is the beer hall of Hitler's famous putsch in 1923, when the Nazi party led by Hitler attempted a coup. Men are in the corner singing songs and raising their beer glasses to a photo of Hitler hanging on the wall. Before today, when Michael came to this place, all he felt was pride. But now he shakes his head. "They've turned this man into their new God, their savior," he mutters.

Michael goes into the phone booth at the end of bar, drops a coin in the slot, and dials a phone number.

The phone rings in the home of Kort Nevaeh and his daughter Kristin. Kort is a handsome man in his late forties. On the wall next to the telephone is a photo of Kort in a World War I German uniform. There is an Iron Cross hanging below the photo. Kort glances at his photo on the wall as he picks up the phone. "Yes? Who is it?"

"Mr. Nevaeh, it's me. Michael. Is Kristin home?"

"Why yes, Michael, she's here. By the way, welcome back home. We were just—"

"Yes," Michael interrupts. "Thanks...I really need to talk to her. Could you please get her for me."

"Why, yes. Is everything all right, Michael?"

"Everything's great...things couldn't be better. Please, I really need to talk to her."

"Hang on. I'll get her."

Kort walks to the bottom of the staircase and calls out, "Kristin, it's Michael on the telephone." Under his breath, he whispers, "People in love."

While waiting in the phone booth, Michael sees Nazi soldiers in black uniforms through the glass. On their caps are shiny skulls. Michael shakes his head. "God, what was I thinking?" he mutters.

"Sweetheart, you're back!" Kristin's gentle voice over the phone makes Michael smile.

"Yes, I'm back," he says, "and I really need to see you tonight. When can we meet?"

"Oh really? I don't know. So tell me, will you be this passionate after we are married?"

"Something has come up, and I really need to talk to you tonight about our wedding plans. I need to..."

"What?" Kristin teases. "Are you breaking our engagement?"

"No! No, of course not. In fact, I love you more than ever... It's just..."

"It's just what?" Kristin teasing voice is gone. "What's going on, Michael? Are you alright?"

"Yes...Yes of course I'm alright. In fact...I feel clearer than ever. I just need to see you. Tonight. I'll tell you all about it then. How about the park at eight?"

"I can't meet you tonight."

"And why not?" Michael's shoulder's tense. What could be more important then getting together?

"I've been working on my father's suit all day. I need to have it done by tomorrow morning. It's for his big meeting. Michael, what's so important that it can't wait one day?"

"I really can't say over the phone." He sighs. "I guess you're right. You're always right, Kristin. One day isn't going to make any real difference."

"What'd you just say?" jokes Kristin. "About me being right? Michael, we must have a bad connection."

Michael chuckles. "You heard me. I do love you. I think I've always loved you and I always will."

"I will always love you too, Michael. I love you with the best kind of love there is."

"Oh really? What kind is that?"

"Well, Mr. Impatience...I guess I'll tell you about it tomorrow morning. If you buy me breakfast. That kind of love should always be talked about in person."

"Alright, if you say so." Michael looks through the glass at another group of men toasting the photo of Hitler with their beers.

"So let's go to our favorite place tomorrow," says Kristin. "You know the one. How about eight?"

"I hope I can wait until then," Michael admits.

"I hope you can too, silly."

"Alright. I'll see you tomorrow morning, but I want to see you tonight...in my dreams." Suddenly Michael wishes he could stay on the phone with Kristin forever. A strange thought pops into his head; he might never see Kristin again. He shakes it away.

On the other end, Kristin gazes uneasily at an oil painting on the wall. It's of a vase of dying yellow roses. "That would be lovely, it's a deal," she says.

"Until then...good bye."

When Kristin hears the click of the phone hanging up, her body quivers. She stares at the painting again. "What was that all about?" she whispers.

Chapter 7

Thirty Pieces of Silver

The same time Michael and Kristin are talking on the phone, Eric is tending to business of his own. With clenched jaw, he strides down a long hall at the main Munich police station. When he reaches the office of his brother, he knocks quickly and lets himself in. Like any Gestapo office, the walls are stark, except for the large portrait of Adolf Hitler on the wall. Gunther is the second most powerful man in the local Gestapo, thanks to his ruthlessness. He is older than Eric by fives years—fatter and more arrogant too.

Sitting behind his big desk, Gunther sneers at Eric. "So you finally decided to visit your old brother. Since you don't even bother to see our mother, how is it that I have the honor of your company?"

"Our dear mother doesn't want to see me," says Eric. "You know that. My wife isn't welcomed in her home. It's been seventeen years and the family still has not forgiven her. If I can forgive Mary, why can't they?"

"So you've really forgiven her?" Gunther asks with a smirk.

Eric cringes, wishing he were somewhere else—anywhere else. He forces himself into the chair in front of Gunther's desk.

"So why are you here?" asks Gunther, crossing his arms. "What do you want from me?"

"It's...uh...Kristin and Kort Nevaeh. I—"

"Spit it out," snaps Gunther. "What about them?"

Eric speaks slowly. "They need to go away."

"Is that right? And just where is it that you would like them to go?"

"You know where. Wherever all the other Jews are going. To hell for all I care."

Gunther scratches his head, then slowly grins. "Oh...I get it. It's Michael. Michael and Kristin. I've seen them together often. Oh my God! That's a good one. The joke is really on you, my brother." He laughs, holding his large belly.

Eric feels his face growing red with anger and embarrassment.

"What is it with you and your family?" asks Gunther. "How ironic it is about Michael and Kristin. Does Michael know about Kort?"

"Of course not. And I swear to God if anyone tells him, I will kill him. I will kill him!"

"Settle down, my brother," says Gunther, waving his hands. "Of course you will. Of course you will. I think I can help you make this happen. Kort is no problem. He is Mischlinge first degree. However Kristin is the legal limit for Jewish ancestry."

Eric's shoulders drop. "There has to be a way," he says in a choked voice. "We have to get rid of her. We have to."

With a smug smile, Gunther steps around his desk and places his hand on Eric's shoulder. "I will help you. But it will cost you, my brother."

"How about thirty pieces of silver since they are both Jewish?"

Gunther clearly thinks this is funny and starts to laugh. "You think that's enough?"

"Just what in the hell do you want, Gunther?"

"You keep the thirty pieces of silver. I'll take your share of our parents inheritance when our mother dies."

Eric glares up at Gunther. Then he swallows and nods his head in agreement.

Chapter 8

You Are Dead to Me

That night, Michael tosses in his sleep, agitated by disturbing dreams. The last dream is the most disturbing of all.

Michael and Kristin are walking in their favorite park. Michael turns to Kristin and kisses her. Kristin gazes at Michael and says, "Good bye Michael. Remember the plan. This was our choice. Please don't blame Eric and Gunther. Until next time, my love." Kristin vanishes. On the ground where Kristin was standing, lies a single yellow rose.

Michael jolts awake in a panic and checks his wristwatch on the nightstand. It's almost 8 AM. He jumps out of bed, throws his clothes on, and hurries down the street to The Three Roses restaurant. He lets out a sigh as he walks through the front door. He's five minutes early. He sits down at a table next to the window and orders a coffee.

Fifty-five minutes later, Michael checks his wristwatch. It's 8:50 AM. Kristin would never be this late. Something had to be horribly wrong. Michael jumps up, knocking over his coffee cup. Coffee spills everywhere. The waitress scowls. Michael throws some money on the table, walks out of the restaurant and towards Kristin's house.

Police sirens blare in the distance. The sound is gone as Michael turns onto Kristin's street. Neighbors have gathered in front of Kristin's home with worried looks. "Oh my God. No!" cries Michael.

He almost knocks two ladies down as he storms up the front steps and into the open door.

The house is a mess. Furniture is knocked over. Clothes are strewn everywhere. Drawers are open, their contents emptied onto the floor. "Kristin! Kristin! Kort! Kort!" Michael yells as he tears from room to room. He knows they're gone. But he can't help himself. "Kristin! Kort!"

In Kristin's room, he stares at a photo on her vanity. It's of Kristin and Michael smiling at each other. Next to the photo is a vase full of dying yellow roses. Michael fingers the dead petals and lets them crumble in his hands. "My God, Kristin, what have they done to you?"

He drops onto the bed, his head in his hands. Who took them away? Where could they be? Could he get them back? Michael knows who has the answers—Uncle Gunther. But Gunther was like his father, both stanch Nazis and haters of Jews. How much help would he be? Michael had to see him; there was no other place to go.

Michael runs out of the house and up the street two blocks to the streetcar. He jumps onto the streetcar and plops on the bench, catching his breath. An old lady sits next to him. Michael glances around at the others on the car. A young soldier has a strange smile on his face, as if he knows something that nobody else does. The faces of almost everyone else look blank. At the very back of the car by themselves is a young teenage couple, in their own little world. The boy teases the girl and when she turns away, he steels a kiss on her cheek. Watching them, Michael's eyes well up. *Kristin. Kristin.*

Suddenly he's heaving soul-rendering sobs. The old lady next to him slides away to the other end of the bench. Others turn their heads away.

Finally, the streetcar arrives at Michael's stop. He staggers off and heads towards the police station. His sobbing has turned to rage. He has to find out who did this. Kristin and Kort's abduction happened within a few hours of his argument with his father. He must be involved. But was his father really capable of ruining his son's life? Maybe it was Gunther. A way to get back at Eric and his family— Gunther never liked Eric. Either way, Gunther was the key. There was no way the police could have done this without Gunther's knowledge. Michael's hands roll into fists as he marches up the steps. Whoever did this will pay.

Inside the police station, Michael barges into Gunther's office. "So where are they? Where are they, you fat bastard?"

Gunther looks up from his papers, then rises to his feet. "Michael...Michael what are you talking about? Where are who?"

Michael walks over to Gunther and grabs the lapels of Gunther's uniform and stares into his eyes. "You know damn well who. Kristin and her father."

Gunther pulls away from Michael and strikes Michael's face with the back of his hand. Michael crashes to the floor. Gunther straightens his police jacket. "I have no idea what you're talking about, you stupid boy!"

Lying in a heap on the floor, Michael shudders. "They're gone," he cries. "They're gone. She is gone."

"You are as weak and disgusting as your father," hisses Gunther. "I don't know where your Jewish friends are; nor do I care. Why don't you ask your father where your girlfriend is?"

Michael pushes himself up from the floor and swipes the tears from his cheeks. "I thought so. My father. What did he do?"

Gunther grins but says nothing.

Michael points his finger at Gunther. "If either of you have caused them harm, I vow I will—"

"Really? What do you vow?"

"I vow...to see you both in hell!" yells Michael. Spit flies out of his mouth.

"Hell?" says Gunther. "Hell is to be married to a Jew in Nazi Germany in 1938. Now get out of my office before you end up in the same place your Jewish friends are going!" He grabs Michael by the arm, throws him out of his office, and slams the door behind him.

"Tell me where they are!" cries Michael, banging on the door.

Gunther opens the door and points a pistol into Michael's face. Then he slowly shuts the door. "You are dead to me, Michael," he says through the closed door, "don't ever come here ever again."

Michael runs out of the police station, down the street, and past an old brick-built Catholic church with twin towers. When he reaches the butcher shop, he blasts through the store, shoving customers and clerks out of his way.

Eric is in the backroom, cutting the head off of a dead pig with a large butcher knife. His white apron is full of blood. He jerks his head up when Michael storms in. "What have you done, Father? Tell me. Now."

Eric's silent icy stare makes Michael's blood boil. He walks over to Eric and punches him with all the force he can muster. Eric falls backwards knocking the dead pig off the table. Then he crumbles to the floor with the pig, and the knife drops out of his hand. Michael grabs the knife off the floor and points it at Eric.

Eric wipes blood from his lip with the back of his hand. His sleeve rises up revealing a tattoo of a rose winding around a dagger in the shape of a large letter E. "What have I done? I have saved you. That is what I have done."

"Saved me? How could this save me? You have taken the love of my life from me. Who knows what horrors Kristin and her father will suffer. All because of you. I hate you. I will always hate you. If it wasn't for my mother and Leni, I would kill you right now! You stupid and foolish old man." Michael pushes the knife closer to Eric's face. "Look at me, look into my eyes. I want you to remember this day forever."

Eric tries to turn away, but Michael pushes the knife closer forcing Eric to look right at him. "I vow today," says Michael, "on everything holy. I will never see you again. You are dead to me. I no longer have a father and you no longer have a son. I will forever hate you. I curse you to a life of pain."

Michael throws the knife on the floor next to Eric's chest. Then he turns and walks out.

Chapter 9

What a Story

A stream of sunlight falls through the open roof of the half destroyed house in Nancy, France, 1944. The rain has stopped for now. "So that's what happened," Michael tells Johan. "All because I didn't listen to Kristin. I didn't listen to myself. Deep down inside I had a feeling about it. In fact, I remember the hair on my arms standing on end when Kristin told me that we needed to leave before it was too late."

"What a story," says Johan.

"How strange, that my whole life came down to the choices I made in just a few minutes. I believed in Hitler then. Or I wanted to. My national pride signed her death warrant. And mine."

"Kristin is dead?"

Michael swallows hard. "I was talking to a soldier in the 12th SS. His brother works in one of those camps where they take the Jews for relocation. Johan, do you know how they relocate the Jews?"

"No."

"They relocate them to the grave yard. The relocation camps are really death camps," says Michael in a weary voice.

"That's impossible. No government could get others to kill helpless people like that, especially women and children"

"Women and children are dying everyday. Leni is dead now too. My mother was badly burned in the same raid. And have you ever thought that every man we kill is someone's child? We drop bombs on their families and they drop bombs on ours. Really, what's the difference between a death camp and an air raid? Everyone is just as dead."

Johan picks up an open can of rations and takes a bite. "My father was in the army and my parents said the army would be a good career for me. Something they could be proud of. I'm not proud of it though."

Michael gives him a sad smile. "Funny. I ended up in the same business as my father too—the butcher business."

"Yes," says Johan. "Our parents are proud of us now. They got their children into the kill-or-be-killed business. Yet for some odd reason they will be so surprised if they get the news that their sons are dead. What did they expect from the killing business? A happy ending?"

"There's only one thing more stupid than the people who send their children to war."

"And what is that?" asks Johan.

"The stupid children that go."

"Amen. But how did you end up here? If you hate war so much."

"I spent months trying to find Kristin. When the war broke out, I was in a jail in Cologne. I broke some guy's nose in a bar fight. The guy turned out to be a friend of the police chief. They said I had two choices. I could either join the army or go to a concentration camp. Looking back I really wish I had gone to the camp. I should have stood up for my views against the war. I took the easy way out and now I'm just a hypocrite."

A hundred yards away, an American soldier, James Muller, stands on a roof overlooking the house where Michael and Johan sit. He's an excellent sniper and a marginal German interpreter. James looks through his riflescope and takes aim on Johan's head. He has a clear shot through the upstairs window. His hands quiver in nervousness, but his face holds a strange smile.

Back in the half destroyed house, Johan gives a soft punch to Michael's shoulder. "Hey, if you'd gone to the camp, you'd have missed the pleasure of my company. And of course—"

Crash! Glass shatters as the bullet shoots through the window and into Johan's head. Michael stares at Johan's lifeless body; blood spurts from his head and half of his face is gone. Michael jerks away and vomits.

More gunfire ricochets from outside. Michael's heart hammers. He grabs his MP 40 machine gun and sprints outside and into the shadow of a nearby building. Two American soldiers run by him on the other side of the street. Michael opens fire with his machine gun. The Americans fall in a dead heap, one on top of the other.

James sees Michael killing the two soldiers and takes a shot at Michael.

The bullet ricochets off the building next to Michael's head. Michael looks up to see James at a window on the second floor of a house across the street. James works the bolt of his rifle as he runs down the stairs. Michael runs to the house and kicks in the front door.

As Michael enters the house, James is waiting for him at the bottom of the staircase. For a split second, their eyes lock. James points his rifle at Michael's stomach. Michael hesitates but James doesn't. He shoots Michael, sending him to the floor. James works the bolt action putting another bullet in the breach, but doesn't shoot Michael again. He walks over to Michael, still pointing his gun at him, and kicks Michael's machine gun out of reach of Michael's hand. Michael's uniform is full of blood.

"Please...please," says Michael in English.

James' mouth falls open. "You speak American?" he asks in German.

"Are you German too?" Michael asks.

"Yeah...so what? I'm an interpreter." James shifts his weight. He doesn't like to talk about his German heritage.

Michael puts his hand in his jacket. James points his rifle at Michael's head. Michael pulls out a photo and stretches out his hand as if to give the photo to James.

"Please..." Michael begs through ragged breaths. "Can you...let her know? My mother...for God's sake."

Michael passes out, dropping his outstretched hand. James pokes Michael with his rifle. Michael's eyes are shut but he is still breathing. James takes the photo from Michael's hand. It's a photo of Mary and Leni, and now has blood on it. James turns it over to see an address and some writing.

Another American soldier hurries into the room. Frank Costello is a cocky New York Italian. James quickly slips the photo into his pocket.

"What's going on here?" asks Frank. "I heard German voices."

"Yes, you did Costello...I speak German, remember? That's my job. I just shot this son of a bitch."

Frank's eyes flare. "Good. We need more of them looking that way. Goddamn Germans. I hate them all!"

"Them all?" James fires back. "Not all Germans are bad. There're good Germans too."

"Yeah? The only good German is a dead one."

"I'm German raised by German Americans. Don't forget Mr. Costello, that the Italians were on the wrong side in this war for awhile too."

"Yeah, so? What does that mean?"

"It means," James says. "My wop friend, go fuck yourself."

Frank glares at James, then turns away and looks at Michael. "Your friend is still breathing." Frank takes his bayonet off of his gun belt, puts it on his M 1 rifle, and plunges the bayonet deep into Michael's chest. Then he puts his foot on Michael's chest and pulls the bayonet out. Michael lets out a gasp. Frank grins at James. "No, Herr Muller, go fuck *yourself!*"

Chapter 10

The Welcome Home Party

Total blackness. Out of the blackness comes the image of Michael and Kristin as they kiss in the park. A yellow rose falls from Kristin's hand to the ground.

Michael's body lies on the cold floor. Frank and James are gone.

A strange white light fills the room. It's coming out of Michael too. Finally his spirit, his actual soul, emerges from his dead body and floats to the ceiling. Michael's spirit gazes in amazement and confusion at the body he left behind. Then he floats out of the house and over the city. Night has fallen. There is lightning and smoke everywhere.

Michael sees the battle raging below. Soldiers on both sides are falling to their demise. The spirits of the dead soldiers float skyward. One dead soldier shoots up from the battle and comes close to Michael. It is Frank Costello. Michael and Frank give each other puzzled looks. Their speed picks up, and they move away from each other and into the black clouds.

Confused and dazed, Michael moves through the clouds and far above planet Earth. As he continues traveling at a remarkable speed, an incredible sense of peace washes over him. The

German uniform is gone; his spirit body is glowing. He sees a bright light more powerful than a million suns, and moves into the middle of the light.

Everything is black.

Michael stands in the middle of the park where he and Kristin used to walk hand in hand. The colors are vibrant. A single yellow rose lies on the pathway next to him. The park and town are deserted.

Elisa, the family cat, is stretched on a park bench. Michael walks over and pets her. "Elisa? What is this place? Where is everyone?"

The cat follows Michael as he wanders out of the park, then out of city. In the distance is a wonderful large country estate. The closer Michael gets, the more he's overtaken by a sweet familiarity. He knows he has been here before. Yet his mind says it's not possible. When Michael gets to the front steps, he turns around—the cat is gone.

Michael walks up to the massive double front doors, over ten feet high. Next to the doors is a sign. "Be careful what you wish for, you just might get it!" Michael laughs out loud. "If this is heaven," he says. "God must have a sense of humor!"

Michael pulls open the doors and finds himself in the lobby of a majestic 1930s movie theater. Warm light pulsates from vintage lighting throughout the lobby. Rich maroon carpets cover the floor, and walnut panels line the walls.

Instead of a ceiling, there is only sky—a view into the universe of planets and suns, swirling galaxies, all in a grand cosmic light show. Michael is blown away.

Suddenly he's aware that hundreds of people are there. It's a huge party. Michael's eyes widen. There is Kristin! Leni is there. So is Johan.

People from the balcony call down to him. "Welcome home, Michael!" Others clap their hands.

Leni waves. Frank grins. Kristin walks towards Michael. She is wearing a long white dress, and is as beautiful as ever. "Kristin," he says, his chest tight. "I thought I'd never see you again."

"Of course you'd see me again," she says, taking Michael by the arm.

"Wh-what is this place?" he asks. "Where are we?"

Kristin kisses him on the cheek and whispers in his ear. "Welcome home, sweetheart."

"Are we in heaven?"

"It goes by many different names."

Johan comes over and gives Michael a big bear hug. "Good to see you, old buddy. What a trip, huh?"

"Uh...I guess," says Michael. "But how did you get here so fast? You died just a couple of minutes ahead of me."

"Not exactly," says Johan. "We died many years ago in Earth time."

"Really? But you did die first, right?"

"Time doesn't always work that way," says Johan. "In fact, there's actually no such thing as Earth time. It doesn't really exist."

Michael rubs the back of his neck. "No time? What in the hell are you talking about?"

"We just use time. For our stories."

"So what am I doing here? What's this all about?"

"It's kind of like a debriefing after a combat mission. Remember those?"

"Yeah."

Johan puts his hand on Michael's shoulder. "Well my friend, you might say this is a debriefing on your mission to one of the toughest places in the entire universe—planet Earth!"

"Come on, Johan," Kristin says, "let Michael catch his breath. He just got here. Give him some time to—"

"Hey," Michael cuts in. "I thought you said there was no such thing as time."

"You're catching on," says Johan. He and Kristin laugh. But Michael just shakes his head.

"I'm going to leave you two love birds alone for now," said Johan. "Michael, I'll catch up with you later...after your life review."

Michael turns to Kristin. "Life review? What is a life review? Why is it that everyone knows what's going on, but me? I seem to be the butt of some kind of huge cosmic joke."

"You'll know everything soon enough," says Kristin, touching Michael's cheek. "In fact, you'll know more then you really want to."

"I want to know everything."

"Of course you do. But the soul can't handle too much information at one time. So remembering who you really are is always a gradual process, otherwise you might get what we call a spiritual meltdown. It's the same reason why you, like many others, don't come directly here after they die."

"So where did I go?"

"It really isn't a place," says Kristin. "It's more like a state of mind or condition. When people go through a lot a trauma before their death or they die a violent death, they need a period of recuperation, where they're washed in love."

"Are there other places you can go after you die?" asks Michael.

"I can't even begin to tell you how many. For each person it's different and no two are the same." A waiter walks by with a tray of champagne glasses. Michael stops him and reaches for two glasses. But before he has a chance to grab them, they float into his waiting hands. He downs one of them, and the instant the glass is empty, it floats back to the tray. "So, you could say this is my own personal heaven."

"It's what you wanted to wake up to Michael, coming out of the dream of your last life."

"Then what about hell?" asks Michael.

"There is really only one true hell. And that hell is to be in a body on Earth and believing your story is totally real."

Michael chews on his lip. "What about the hell the churches talk about?"

"Since some people want to believe that's where they're going when they die, that's exactly what they get," says Kristin. "Remember what the sign said on the front door? Be careful for what you wish for—"

"You just might get it!"

"Except, here you *always* get it," Kristin says. "That's why it's called heaven. You always get whatever your heart desires."

"Whew. This is a lot to take in," says Michael. He downs the other glass of champagne. The glass floats away. "That's really good champagne."

"The best," says Kristin.

"But I don't feel any effects from the alcohol."

"Of course not. There's no need here."

"So I can drink as much as I like?"

Kristin leads Michael into the crowd. "That's right. Now let's go have fun. This is your welcome home party after all."

A man steps up and shakes Michael's hand. "Welcome back, Michael. Good to see you my old friend."

"Kort? You're here too?"

"Of course."

"I'm so happy to see you both alive," says Michael. "I always wondered what happen to you and Kristin after my bastard father sold you both out?"

Kort frowns. "Your bastard father? Kristin, you haven't told him about Eric yet?"

"I was waiting for the right—"

"Forget about my miserable father," snaps Michael. "What happened to you?"

"Well Michael," Kort begins. "I would have to say it was one of the most horrific experiences I ever had to go through. We were both sent to a death camp called Dachau. Kristin and I both died unspeakable deaths."

A shudder passes through Michael. "I feared as much. I'm so sorry. I'll do everything I can to get justice for you both."

Kort's face is calm. "Justice is a strange thing. Remember it is written 'Judge not lest thee be judged.'"

"What does that mean?"

Kort squeezes Michael's hand. "Maybe it means that things are not always as they appear."

"Well, I never thought heaven would be like this."

"You have just come from the illusion of one of your many stories," says Kort. "It was no more real than a Hollywood movie set."

Michael shakes his head in disbelief.

"Yes my friend," Kort says. "Our stories can be very confusing, crazy, and sometimes even scary. When people are in their stories, they react to everything that happens to them in one of two ways: love or fear. On Earth most people choose fear. As I have done so many times myself. In fact, the time period we lived in on Earth was known as 'The Age of Fear' and it'll be known that way for decades to come."

"Wow," says Michael. "The Age of Fear. That explains a lot. But Kort, you couldn't ever choose fear over love. You've always been one of the kindest men I've ever known."

"If only that were true. I still have a lot of things to work out, as you will see later."

"Yes, don't we all," says Kristin.

A voice booms down from the balcony. "May I have your attention, please!"

Michael looks up and flinches when he sees the booming voice is Eric's. "What the hell is he doing here?"

"You'll understand soon," says Kristin.

The crowd grows quiet. Michael's hands roll into fists while Eric goes on with his announcement. "It is so good to be with old friends again. And I'm sure I speak for everyone here that it warms our hearts to see Michael again. My very dear friend."

"Dear friend?" growls Michael. "Is he mad? I would have had no problem killing that old bastard. If only I had the chance."

"Shhh," said Kristin.

Eric continues. "Everyone is dying, and forgive the pun, to see his life review. So please could you all come to the main auditorium. Get your popcorn and refreshments in the lobby if you like. The life review will begin shortly."

"Eric is coming to my life review?" asks Michael. "This can't be heaven. It feels more like—"

"Michael," says Kristin. "Calm down. You'll understand once we do your life review."

"I'm not going to some kind of movie where everyone gets to sit around and eat popcorn and pick my life apart."

"Part of the fun of this whole thing is—"

"Fun?" Michael snaps. "The life I just had was many things, but fun was not one of them. My life was a big—"

"As I was saying," interrupts Kristin. "Part of the fun of this whole experience is letting people see how in retrospect their life went...with no, and I repeat, no judgment. From anyone."

"Yeah, right. Like that can ever happen."

Kristin sighs. "There's only one person that can ever judge you and your life plan and that person will always be you. "

"You and everyone here are nuts," says Michael. "There was no life plan—no design to my life. All twenty-four years of it was total chaos from start to finish. And in fact—"

"It's funny," says Kristin. "For someone who has been here in heaven just a few minutes, you're so sure of how this whole thing works."

"So you think I'm arrogant and too sure of myself?"

"No, Michael. That would be a label and a judgment. Words, however, have power. They can hurt and even kill. Let me show you the power of words."

Kristin snaps her fingers. Instantly, Kristin and Michael are in the park in Munich, watching themselves in 1939. Michael is telling her about Hitler. "There's no way it will ever happen. Look how Hitler brought this country out of the depression, in just a few years. Germany is now one of the strongest countries in the world. Hitler doesn't want war. No sane man wants war. Not after the carnage of the last one. I'm sure he's a man of peace. You must believe me."

Kristin snaps her fingers again and they are both back at the party in the movie theater. "Michael, do you know what I did after you said those words?"

"No."

"I put my life in your hands, and in a way my father's life too. And you know the price we all paid for that."

Kristin places her hands on both sides of Michael's face. "I love you. I have always loved you. But sometimes you don't know what in the hell you're talking about, and this is one of them. You hate Eric so much because you think he betrayed my father and me. But it was you, Michael. You betrayed me way before Eric ever did!"

Michael twists his face out of Kristin's hand. "How could you say such a thing? I love you so much, I would have done any—"

"Oh yes! You loved me. But you loved something even more."

"There was nothing in the world I loved more then you."

"That's an easy thing to say now," says Kristin. "You'll soon see you've always been more loyal to your own opinion and your politics, than any woman in your life."

"I just..."

"This isn't the first time either," says Kristin. "This whole love and loyalty thing is something you and I have been working on for many lifetimes. It's not just the fact you chose your country over me again. It's the fact that you promised yourself that you would never go to war ever again for any country."

"I did that? I made that promise?"

"You'll remember soon enough."

Michael lets out a long breath.

Kristin takes Michael by the hand. "There is something else you're going to remember real soon too. It's about Eric, the person you seem to hate so much. Eric is really..."

Chapter 11

Your Crazy Life

Eric, Gunther, and Leni peer over the balcony at the crowd below. When Leni spots Michael and Kristin, she elbows Gunther. "What do you think's going on with Michael down there?"

Gunther taps Eric on the shoulder and points in the direction of Michael. "Looks like Michael's getting ready to have a meltdown," says Gunther. "I sure hope Kristin isn't telling him too much before the life review."

"We should get this review going before it's too late," says Eric. He clears his throat and shouts over the crowd. "Last chance to find your seats, friends. The review will begin in three Earth time minutes." With eager faces, people head up the spiral staircase.

Michael and Kristin look up at the balcony, then at each other.

"Darling," says Kristin, "it's time for us to see what really happened down there on Earth. We are about to see the big picture, as they say. It's time to remember who we really are."

"Big picture? Does that mean we can see what could have happened if we had made different choices?"

"You mean like all the different possibilities?" Kristin asks. "Just the fun ones, like going to America, our marriage, our children and..."

Michael puts four fingers over Kristin's mouth, as if to say, please say no more.

Kristin takes Michael by the arm. Together they head up the stairs, through giant golden doors, and into the main auditorium. Constellations of stars sparkle everywhere.

"Oh my God!" says Michael.

Kristin smiles. "I thought you didn't believe in God."

"I don't know what to believe."

"Well there is a god. Who do you think thought all this up? God loves to surprise all of us. Especially those who like to jump to wrong conclusions. Do you know of anyone like that?"

"If I can't keep up with you, what chance would I have with God?"

Michael looks past the rows and rows of seats at an enormous movie screen. It stretches from the high ceiling to the floor. Gold panels and colorful gemstones surround it. "That's for my life review?"

"Yes," says Kristin. She gestures to all the people standing by their seats, their faces turned to Michael. "They're waiting for you."

As Michael and Kristin step down the aisle, everyone applauds. "They're treating me like I'm some kind of famous movie director," Michael mutters. He shyly waves to everyone, then quickly settles into his seat next to Kristin.

The lights dim and dramatic music plays. "This is Your Crazy Life" blazes across the screen. As the words and music fade, Michael appears on the screen wearing a Roman toga. "Greetings to you all," he says. "I just want to thank everyone for helping me put this life plan together. I especially want to thank those of you who were key players in my story."

Michael shifts in his seat. "Just when did I say this anyway?" he whispers to Kristin.

"Before your last incarnation on Earth. Now hush!"

The Michael on the screen continues. "Michael, you are probably leaning over to Kristin right about now and asking her what is going on here. Since I am you, let me just say please sit back and enjoy the show. This is your Earth story 11,777. All your questions will be answered in due time and you will remember everything about your preexistence."

Michael clutches the arms of his seat. "Oh my God! We have to stop this whole thing, right now."

"Why?" asks Kristin. "Are you okay? What's wrong?"

"I forgot my popcorn!" Michael laughs.

"Stop it," scolds Kristin. "I should come back as your mother next time, just so I can give you a good spanking."

Michael grins and sinks back in his seat. He focuses back at the screen just as Michael on the screen starts to speak again. "The first thing we are going to see is our group's life plan. Then my own personal life plan. Then how it actually played out together this time around. We'll see all the usual fun and ugly stuff. The insane relationships, the stupid politics and religions...and how they all fit into this whole crazy thing we love to do."

In his seat, Michael turns to Kristin. "The fun and ugly stuff of relationships?"

Kristin puts her elbow into Michael's ribs. "Hush!"

Back on the screen, Michael continues. "We all know that the group's karma started many lifetimes ago. Let's take a look at a few clips from those lifetimes. This will help us put things into perspective about what happened in our last life. So friends, sit back and enjoy."

The screen comes to life with photos of ancient Egypt. On screen Michael starts narrating. "This was a very interesting time period, with the power struggle between the priesthood and ruling class." A rapid progression of many scenes flashes on the screen, with thousands of years passing in only a few minutes.

Then the screen shows photos of ancient Rome with Michael and Kristin dressed in Roman garments. Kristin in her seat whispers into Michael's ear. "Remember this one? This is where I betrayed you."

Michael keeps his eyes fixed on the screen. "Hush!"

Soon the scenes shift to more modern days. One shows Eric killing Frank Costello in World War I. Then the movie jumps to a scene of Michael as a small boy, sitting on Eric's knee, laughing.

Michael's chest squeezes. That was the moment he felt the closest to his father.

Soon there's a scene of Michael kissing Kristin in the park. In their seats, Michael and Kristin smile at each other. Michael sees others in the audience smiling too.

The scene changes to Michael's pro-Hitler speech to Kristin in the park. "Hitler doesn't want war. No sane man wants war. Not after the carnage of the last one. I'm sure he's a man of peace. You must believe me." Everyone in the audience laughs. For a moment Michael cringes in embarrassment, then he laughs too.

The next scene shows Michael and Eric in the butcher shop.

Michael's hand flies to his mouth as he hears himself on screen. "Saved me? How could this save me? You have taken the love of my life from me. Who knows what horrors Kristin and her father will suffer. All because of you. I hate you. I will always hate you. If it wasn't for my mother and Leni, I would kill you right now! You stupid and foolish old man."

Scenes speed up. Muffled voices from the screen fill the auditorium. Some of the voices are full of anger, others full of love. People in the audience laugh one minute, and become quiet the next.

Finally it's over and the music begins again, softer this time. Michael sits in his seat stunned. To his surprise, Kristin and the audience rise to give him a standing ovation. Voices ring out. "Bravo, Michael!" "Well done!"

Michael and Kristin sit in their seats while others file out of the auditorium. "Wow! What a story," says Michael. "But I don't understand why everyone liked it. They even liked me. I was such a jerk. I did awful things."

Kristin touches Michael on the arm. "But, did you try your best, Michael?"

"Well yes, I guess but—"

"Do you remember what I said? That there would be no judgment here."

"But wouldn't this be the place to be judged? Remember the men I killed and what I did to you and your father?"

"No one can judge you, because they would have to judge themselves too. Those two men you killed tortured you to death in the Spanish inquisition. Remember what Kort said? 'Judge not lest thee be judged."

"I thought Jesus said those words."

"Actually, Kort was Jesus in another lifetime."

Michael's eyes widen. "Really?"

"Just kidding, of course."

"I'm being serious here," says Michael. "Don't we have to pay for our sins in some way?"

"You are so cute when you're trying to be serious. Do you know what the word sin means?"

Michael shakes his head no.

"Its translation means to miss the mark of perfection. Wouldn't you say every one of us has missed the mark of perfection in one way or another in our lifetimes on Earth?"

"I guess."

"And Michael, who do you think was in the most pain watching that life review, anyway?"

"Me, for sure"

"So there you have it. You've paid the price for your sins—your imperfection—with your own condemnation. You've been and always will be your own worse critic for yourself and the stories you create. The never ending story of Michael."

"So my lifetimes are stories I'm creating? Like movies featuring me?"

"Yes. In your stories, you play a major role. In other people's stories, you might be just an extra, with a small part. In this last story, you were the scriptwriter and main character."

"So you guys were just characters in my story?"

Kristin nods. "This time I was the lover, and Eric was—"

"The villain!"

"That's right. You needed a villain and your best friend Eric volunteered for the part."

Michael scans the auditorium, and spots Eric standing at the very top of the aisle. Eric is grinning from ear to ear. "Oh my God," says Michael. "Eric!"

"Yes, Eric your closest friend," says Kristin.

Michael dashes up the aisle to Eric. "It was you," Michael says.

"No, Michael, it was you." Michael and Eric embrace. Then Michael says. "I guess you're right."

"Yes, it was your story this time," says Eric. "But I helped."

"So, it was you and I? We made the whole strange story up?"

"There were others that helped too. We all had ideas to make the story better...crazier."

"Unbelievable."

"How did you like my performance?" asks Eric with a smirk. "I thought I did a great job as a bad guy. What do you think, Academy Award material?"

"You were such a great villain. I really hated you."

"You needed someone to betray you, so you could have an opportunity to forgive. It was a really tough story that few people could have done at all. But you wanted a hard story."

"Just like any good video game—the harder ones are a lot more fun?"

"We all like a good challenge, don't we?" says Eric.

Michael grins and gives Eric a high five. On Eric's forearm is the tattoo of a rose winding around a dagger in the shape of a large letter E.

"But why is it," asks Michael, "that we can't remember our past lives when we are in the game?"

"A good actor doesn't play the role, but becomes the person he is playing. Like any good actor, we must be able to forget who we really are on the stage of life. That's why when we are born we have temporary amnesia. Sometimes small children will remember for a few years, but after awhile they forget too."

"I get it," says Michael. "We have to forget so we can believe the stories are real. That's what makes the whole thing work. We have to forget who we really are."

"And who are we really, Michael?"

The corners of Michael's mouth slowly curl

upward. "I remember now. We are spiritual beings having a physical experience."

"Yes, we are all born into forgetfulness and spend the rest of our lives trying to regain our true consciousness."

Kristin appears at their side. "Alright guys, don't you think we've had enough of the deep conversations for one night?"

"We're in night time?" Michael says. "I thought there was no such thing as time."

"Michael," Kristin huffs playfully. "I've had about enough of you. Now let's get back to your welcome home party. If not, we can always watch your life review again..."

"I think I'd rather take a beating, than do that."

"Good, let's go," says Eric. "We can start talking about our next trip to Earth."

Michael blinks. "You're kidding. Kristin, he's kidding, right?"

Kristin takes Eric by one arm and Michael by the other. Michael shakes his head. "And, I thought you two were my friends."

Eric grins at Michael. "Payback can be a bitch!"

"Really, Eric?" Michael grins. "Well, I can't wait to get you on the receiving end next time!"

"Oh really, we'll just see about that."

The three of them walk through the giant golden doors out of the auditorium, down the stairs, and back into what should be the lobby area. The lobby is gone now. Instead, the room is a magnificent ballroom with a vaulted glass ceiling.

Chapter 12

The Vacation Life

Music and laughter swirl through the ballroom. Food and drink are everywhere. Johan sits with Gunther at a table in the corner. A large holographic cube, full of squares and game pieces, hovers between them. With his finger, Johan directs one of his game pieces—a snow leopard—onto a new square. "So Gunther, old buddy, do you have anything lined up for your next lifetime yet?"

Gunther grins. "You're going to think I'm a wimp. But I'm going for a nice, easy trip this time."

Johan rolls his eyes. "Sure you are."

"No really. That last trip to Earth was pretty rough. I need a vacation lifetime next."

"Vacation life," snorts Johan. "Yeah, right."

"So what? Do you want to hear about my next life or not?"

"Okay, tell me about your next easy life. I'm all ears."

Gunther blinks his eyes at the game cube and one of his pieces—a dragon—leaps two squares. "I'm going to have all the usual stuff that any good vacation life has. I want the pretty trophy wife and two perfect kids. Of course, lots of money. I want the great big house in Hollywood. I will have a big black S.U.V. that gets only six miles to the gallon, and of course there will be—"

"No real problems," says Johan. "How do you expect to grow without problems?"

"I'll be growing, just at a slower pace. There'll be some problems."

"No problems...no growth. And as we all know, no pain...no gain."

"What's the big hurry? We have all of eternity to play with. It seems that everyone here is trying to out do each other on how interesting and insane they can make their next story."

"Hey, we all love a good story but there is more to it than that. What better way to find out who we really are, then when the chips are down, so to speak? It's so easy to say grand things in heaven where everything is perfect." Johan changes his voice to a women's voice. "I would never betray you. I would die first."

Gunther chuckles.

Johan's voice changes back to his own. "Or even the most famous line there is—and everyone says it at least once a life time. "I will love you forever no matter what!"

"That's true," says Gunther. "Here in perfection and with perfect hindsight, it's easy to say all those grand things."

"All of us living here in perfection brag about all those wonderful things we would do for each other, if we only had the chance."

"Then, you get dropped into a body. You forget who you really are. Your crazy story begins. And your story turns into your own private hell."

Johan moves a piece in the game cube and vaporizes Gunther's dragon.

"Good move," says Gunther.

"But," says Johan, "the funniest thing in the universe is how people curse God for their crazy and insane lives."

Gunther makes a move in the game cube and vaporizes three of Johan's pieces. "Touché!" says Johan.

"And of course in the end," says Gunther, "the big surprise is the whole thing was our own idea. God had nothing to do with our story. God just made it possible to live it and learn from it."

Johan surveys the damage on the game board. "What's really nuts is when we get bored, we all go back and do it some more."

"What else are we going to do with eternity?"

Both Gunther and Johan laugh. "True. So Gunther did you say an S.U.V.?"

"Yeah, so?"

"Sports Utility Vehicles weren't around until the eighties. So, let me guess, you want to be born in the United States in the late nineteen sixties. That way you'll be old enough to drive when S.U.V.s are around."

"Good guess. Late sixties or maybe even early seventies."

"Our group is going to be in the sixties too," says Johan. "But we'll all be getting born in late forties or early fifties, so that we'll be old enough for the fun part—drugs, sex, and rock and roll. It's going to be one hell of a trip."

"Sounds like it," says Gunther.

"Yeah," says Johan. "It'll make the World War II lifetime seem like a walk in the park. It really gets crazy when we get into our late fifties and sixties around 2021."

"So, let me guess, love, lust, betrayal, and major earth changes—all the usual mayhem?"

"Beats sitting on your fat ass with your trophy wife in Beverly Hills eating sushi!"

Leni instantly appears in front of the table. She's juggling three chrome orbs without actually touching them. "Have either of you guys seen Frank?"

"Hey," says Gunther, "you're a perfect spirit creature and you can't find some guy at a party?"

"Just because you're dead doesn't make you're brilliant," says Leni. "Look at you, Mr. I-want-a-vacation life."

Leni and Johan laugh.

Gunther's face gets red. "Oh, really? How did you find out about that?"

"You posted it on the information board. It said you're looking for a dumb, but good-looking model to be your next wife in California."

"Want to go back and give it a whirl?" asks Gunther. "There'll be lots of money involved. Fame too. Plus I'll be one of the best looking guys in Hollywood."

"Me?" huffs Leni. "Be your wife? I'd rather go back to World War II and die in a bombing again. Don't you remember the last time we got married? Thank God I don't have to work out any more karma with you."

"Was it that bad?" asks Gunther sheepishly.

"Now let me see, are you talking about the

lifetime in Spain or the one in China—the one where I was one of your four wives and you were very fat and had really bad breath."

"Huh?"

Leni smiles. "That's what I thought."

Gunther stands and takes a couple of steps away from them. "I guess I'll be leaving!"

"Hey, Gunther old buddy," says Leni. "I'll tell you what I'll do for you. I'm going to have two kids in my next life. You can be one of them. Then you can see what karma is really all about."

"What do you mean?" Gunther keeps backing away.

"Let's just say, my days of me picking up your dirty underwear are over—forever."

Gunther scowls. "Thanks, Leni, maybe next time."

"That's what I'm talking about," says Leni. "There isn't going to be a next time with us. We're all done with our karma."

"As you wish," says Gunther stiffly. He snaps his fingers once and the game cube disappears. He snaps his fingers twice and he disappears.

Leni turns to Johan. "You know, that guy never did have much of a sense of humor, dead or alive. Remember when he was Hitler's grandmother?"

"Yeah, she was—I mean he was—a real sweetheart."

"What do you think about this next trip," asks Leni. "The one Eric and the boys are cooking up? It sounds like fun, but I was talking to some of the others. They think we're crazy for going back to Earth so soon." She leans closer. "Lets face it, of all the places in the universe, Earth is probably the craziest place to go. There's another planet in the Pleiades that's pretty rough too. What's it called?"

"Ortakeus," Johan says.

"Yeah, that's one of the more fun and insane places to go too."

"You'd have to be nuts to go there. I'll take Earth any day. With all that duality on Earth, you got your male and female thing, then you got your different nationalities—"

"Don't forget the politics."

"Yeah. Then to make the whole thing completely nuts, drop in thousands of different religions, stir in millions of mindless people. Wow. Now you have the universe's biggest, craziest party."

"Maybe they should call Earth the party planet."

"Whatever they call it, I know one thing—I'm kind of an Earth junkie. Earth is my drug of choice."

Leni waves her hand and the three orbs she was playing with become three cats. They look at each other and creep away. "What better place to find out about the biggest mystery in the universe?"

"What would that be?"

"Who are we really? And why do we do the crazy things we do to ourselves and each other?"

Eric steps up to Leni and Johan somehow balancing three foaming glass mugs in his hands.

Leni holds out her hand and one mug drifts into it. She takes a big swig. "Thanks, Eric. I was just thinking I wanted a beer."

"I know," he says. "I heard you."

Johan flicks his fingers and a mug snaps into his hand. "Yeah, thanks, Eric."

Eric drinks from his beer mug. "I was just talking to Gunther. So, Leni, you don't want to be Gunther's wife again?"

"Eric, why don't you be his wife? I think you're more his type. Besides I'm going back as a male next time."

"Does Michael know about our plan to head back to Earth?" asks Johan.

"Not yet. In the life review it hinted that we would all be going back very soon, to work out more of our issues."

"Yeah," Johan says. "I think I'm scheduled for Germany again, nineteen fifty one, the same year as Michael."

"How about you, Leni?" asks Eric.

"I'm nineteen fifty three, Southern California."

"I think this next trip is going to be one of our best yet," Eric says.

A grin stretches across Johan's face. "I can't wait to see the look on Michael's face when he gets the news."

Eric clinks his mug with Johan and Leni's. "Me neither."

Chapter 13

The Choice

A few Earth days later, Kristin, in her long white flowing dress, moves swiftly through the movie theater lobby. Just as she steps onto the spiral staircase, Eric appears instantly before her. "Kristin," he says, grabbing her arm. "He's not going to back out again, is he?"

"No, Eric." Kristin wrestles her arm free. "He won't. Trust me."

"But he's up there. In the auditorium. Watching the whole bloody mess again."

"He'll be fine," says Kristin in a soothing voice. "I promise."

A black cat patters over, and Kristin kneels down to pet it.

"I hope you're right," says Eric. "Michael is one of the key players. We need him to make the story work."

"I know. I know. I'll talk to him. He'll—"

"The timing is perfect. You know Michael must be the first to go."

Kristin turns to Eric. "I know. Trust me. He'll go." She heads up the staircase.

Eric shakes his head, and he and the cat vanish.

Dramatic music and voices echo from above as Kristin climbs the stairs. At the top of the landing she faces the two massive golden doors. With a sigh, she opens the doors and walks into the main auditorium.

Halfway down from the top, Michael slouches in his seat, watching the scenes on the screen.

Michael and Kristin are making love. Michael declares his undying love for her.

Michael waves his hand and the scene changes.

Michael as a young boy is sitting on his father's lap. Both Eric and Michael are laughing.

Michael waves his hand again.

Kristin and Michael are kissing in a park. Kristin lets one yellow rose drop out of her hand to the ground.

Michael wipes a tear from his eyes. Kristin at the top of the balcony wipes away tears too. Michael waves his hand again.

Michael with a knife in his hand is screaming and threatening his father, Eric.

Michael shakes his head and waves his hand again.

Kristin walks down the aisle to Michael and puts her arms around his shoulders. "Oh my God,

Michael, I can't believe you're watching all this again." She waves her hand. The music stops.

"The more I watch what happened down there last time," says Michael, "the more I think we're crazy to go back."

"What? And miss all the fun? I'm going back; we all are. We need you. The whole thing wouldn't be as good without you. The timing is perfect."

Michael waves his hand at the screen, and the scenes stop. "I can't go through this again."

"Please, Michael, I know you can do it this time. You can't back out now. We're all counting on you. *I'm* counting on you."

Michael gazes into Kristin's eyes and sighs. "I know. But couldn't we at least tone it down a bit?"

Kristin laughs. "Tone it down?"

"Hey, I'm the first one to admit it. I bit off way more than I could chew. We made the story way too tough last time."

"Let's face it. We all thought it was a good plan. Otherwise we would've never tried it in the first place."

Kristin waves her hand. They are instantly transported out of the auditorium and into a beautiful rose garden full of yellow roses. Kristin touches one of the roses. It breaks apart and the petals fall into her palm. She shakes her head at the broken flower.

"You see, Michael, it could have turned out very differently. You had a real opportunity to forgive Eric and the others. But you went to war, the one thing you hate the most. That story is over now.

We've all learned from it. Now it's time to prove we can be different. Come on, Michael, one more time?"

Michael touches a rose. It too crumbles in his hand. "How many times have I fallen into the trap of patriotism? How many wars has it been? How many people have I killed, just because some government, some church, some politician said so? Me and my strange idea of loyalty. And this last time with the Nazis and World War II...my God, what a fool I was."

Kristin snaps her fingers and they're back in the auditorium, sitting in seats close to the screen. "This time I know you can do it, Michael," she says. "I know we can do it. This will be the lifetime of true forgiveness. No more war. No more killing."

Michael nods. "You're right, I think. Now that I've forgiven the one person that has been the most difficult to forgive, the rest should be easy!"

"And who would that be?"

"Me."

Kristin leans over and hugs him. "Are you ready to go back with us, my love?"

"Yes, let's go do this."

"Alright, but remember don't forget about the yellow roses."

Michael takes Kristin by the hand and winks. They are instantly outside the movie theater, standing in front of a different set of golden doors. Michael pushes the door open. There is only white light.

Chapter 14

Back in the Insanity

A cluster of shooting stars sails towards planet Earth. One flies through the clouds, somewhere over Los Angeles, California.

It's 1951, and Vivian, a young woman, has been in labor for two days at Queen of Angels Hospital in Los Angeles. When her first child is finally born, the doctor holds the baby boy up by his feet and gives his butt a slight slap. The baby starts to cry—a mournful cry.

A new life has entered the stage. Michael is back.

Three years later, Vivian is back in the hospital ready to deliver her second child.

Again, shooting stars sail towards planet Earth. One of them flies through the clouds, somewhere over Los Angeles. The baby is born.

Another life has entered the stage. Leni is back.

A few days later, three-year-old Michael peers at his new baby brother, Lenny Muller, sleeping in his crib.

Michael recognizes his old friend who was his sister in his last life. *How was the trip?* Michael asks telepathically.

"Burp."

Michael nods. *I know what you mean. You forget what it's like to get into one of these bodies again.*

Lenny continues to sleep with a smile on his face.

Well, Lenny, you wanted to be a male this time. I hope it works out for you.

Vivian steps into the bedroom, and Lenny opens his eyes and gurgles. "Michael," says Vivian as she picks up Lenny, "what do you think of your new baby brother? I was really hoping for a girl, but he'll do just fine."

He'll do? Michael thinks. *That's just great!*

Vivian sits down in a rocking chair and holds Lenny close.

Michael smiles at Vivian. *I like him...or her... or whatever he is. In fact we're old friends.*

Lenny turns his head toward Michael. *Hey, good to see you buddy.*

Good to see you too, Lenny. What do you think of our mother?

I guess she'll do.

I know what you mean. She's pretty unconscious. She and Dad don't know that we understand every word they say, no matter how old we are.

Vivian unbuttons her blouse and starts to breast feed Lenny.

Lenny, your one lucky guy! There's nothing better than a mother's milk and it comes in two very attractive containers.

Lenny is practically getting suffocated because of Vivian's large breasts. *This is sick!*

Michael heads out of the bedroom. *Welcome to the wonderful world of mammals.*

Chapter 15

Isn't Love Grand

Eight-year-old Michael sits on the living room rug in front of the black and white television at home in Pasadena, California. His eyes remain glued to the old World War II movie. As soon as it's over, he grabs his favorite toys—plastic World War II soldiers. "Lenny!" he shouts. "Let's play war."

Lenny runs in and snatches an American toy soldier. Michael makes a German toy soldier jump in front of Lenny's.

"Bang, bang," says Lenny, pretending to shoot. "I hate you. You Nazi!"

Michael's soldier falls over. Lenny moves his solider right over Michael's and points his gun at his chest. Michael pleads. "Don't shoot me. Please, don't shoot me!"

Lenny grins as he shoots the German soldier. "Bang, bang!"

The front door bursts open, startling Michael and Lenny. James Muller, in a gray business suit with a loosened tie around his neck, walks in and glares at the two boys. Then he throws his briefcase in the big black leather chair.

"What's the matter, Daddy?" asks Michael.

James says nothing as he stomps past them and into the kitchen. "Vivian," he yells. "Vivian where the hell are you?"

Vivian hurries in from the backyard. A few clothespins are clipped to her apron. "I'm hanging clothes to dry," she says. "What is it?"

"God damn it. I need a drink." James sits at the kitchen table.

"Okay. Okay. Just relax. Everything will be fine, just tell me all about it." Vivian gathers gin and vermouth from the cupboard, olives from the refrigerator, and ice from the freezer.

"It's those bastards at the office. They're doing it again."

Vivian shakes up the gin, vermouth, and ice in a vintage martini shaker. Then pours the mixture into a martini glass. "What are they doing?"

"Cutting my territory. How in God's name can I make ends meet? When every time I turn around I get a knife in my back?"

"You poor thing." Vivian drops an olive into the martini and hands it to James. "Here you go." She settles into a chair next to him.

James takes a big drink. "Days like this I wish I had stayed in the Army. I would have been a master sergeant by now."

"What's so great about being a master sergeant?"

"Everyone respects you, plus you get to boss people around."

"Honey, you do that now."

James scowls. "Very funny."

Lenny dashes into the kitchen, happily carrying a big baby doll. "Jesus. H. Christ!" yells James. "What in the hell is this?" He swipes the doll out of Lenny's hands and throws it back into the living room.

Lenny cries.

"God damn it," snarls James. "As if my life isn't bad enough. Now I have a god damn fag for a son. Stop that crying. Or I'll give you something to cry about." He slaps Lenny on the leg, which makes Lenny cry harder.

Vivian kneels down and gathers Lenny into her arms. "James A. Muller," snaps Vivian, "how could you? He's just a boy."

James points to Michael, who has just come in with an army helmet on his head and toy gun in his hand. "Look at him, he's my little man. Michael, you're going to be a man when you grow up. Not some little girl like your brother, aren't you?"

Michael shakes his head no.

James' face grows red. He turns to Vivian. " I know you always wanted a girl, but I'm not having any sissy boys in this house. I'll make men out of these boys if it kills me. Just where in the hell did he get that doll from anyway?"

"I guess one of the neighbor girls left it over here when the kids were playing."

Lenny squirms out of Vivian's arms and runs back into the living room with Michael. Vivian stands with her hands on her hips. "You better start treating those boys better, James. Or you'll wish you were back in the army peeling potatoes."

James downs the rest of his martini, and then jumps to attention and salutes Vivian. "Yes sir, Captain. You're the boss."

Vivian can't help herself. She starts to laugh. "I'm glad we got that straight."

James kisses her and puts his hand on her butt and gives it a squeeze. Vivian doesn't seem to mind. "How about another martini, Captain?" he asks.

Vivian gives James a wink. "Coming right up, Sargent."

Michael sticks his head around the corner and gazes at his parents. *Ah...isn't love grand? And to think I picked these two people to be my parents!*

Chapter 16

Break on Through

"Hell NO...we won't go! Hell NO...we won't go!" A stream of students marches through a small college campus in Southern California. "Hell NO...we won't go! Hell NO...we won't go!" Twenty-year-old Michael leads the way, pumping a sign in the air. It reads "End the War in Vietnam NOW!" He painted the words himself that morning. At Michael's side is his friend Kirk Goldman. Kirk was Kort Nevaeh in Michael's last life.

The chant dies down, and Kirk shouts to Michael above the crowd noise. "This war is such fucking bull shit."

"All wars are fucking bull shit," Michael shouts back.

The marchers reach the square in front of the administration building and gather around to hear speakers. The crowd swells with more and more protesters. Police officers with shields form a line.

"Hell NO...we won't go! Hell NO...we won't go!" The students chant louder than before.

Police officers move into the crowd with their clubs raised. Some protesters run. Michael and others try to stand their ground.

"You fucking draft dodging commie bastards," yells a police officer. He is one of the American soldiers Michael killed in World War II. The officer shoves Kirk to the ground. Kirk gets up with a stunned look on his face.

"Fuck you and your war," says Michael.

"Yeah, you fucking Nazi," says Kirk. "Why don't you find some women and children to kill?"

The officer raises his club. "The only people I want to kill are you two faggots."

"Well," fires Michael, "since you're dying to kill something, maybe today's your lucky day."

Suddenly water is everywhere. Police are spraying the crowd with fire hoses. Protesters drop their signs and scatter with the police in hot pursuit. Kirk runs into the street.

Michael races to his 1970 Dodge Challenger convertible in the school parking lot. Since the top is down, he jumps into the drivers seat without opening the car door. He starts up the engine and lays rubber as he zooms out of the parking lot. He gives the police "the finger" as he leaves them in the dust.

Michael cruises down the San Bernardino Freeway. He picks up an eight-track tape off the passenger seat and drops it in his tape deck. Jim Morrison's wild voice booms out the song "Break on Through to the Other Side." Michael is euphoric. He drives down the freeway, wind in his hair, singing Jim's song. It was as if Jim was singing just to Michael.

A few minutes later, Michael steers his car into the driveway of an old two-story home in Azusa. His parents had sold the little house in Pasadena after Vivian's mother passed away, and bought this one. An American flag hangs from the house. Michael gets out of the car and salutes the flag with a sneer.

As Michael walks up to the house, the family's cat greets him. Music echoes from the open kitchen window. It's Frank Sinatra's song "If You're Young at Heart." Michael circles around to the back porch and opens the screen door to the kitchen.

Chapter 17

Frank Sinatra's Music

Vivian carefully pulls cake layers out of the oven and places them on cooling racks on the table. Then she wipes her hands on her pretty pink apron.

From the doorway, Michael shakes his head at the half-empty wine bottle sitting on the counter.

Vivian seems in a dream world, humming to Frank Sinatra's silky voice. She gathers cans of icing and sits at the table. Her back is to Michael, but somehow she senses his presence. "Michael, where have you been?" she asks without turning around.

"Out changing the world, Mom."

"That's nice sweetheart," says Vivian. "I'm making a three-layered vanilla cake. What kind of icing do you want—chocolate or vanilla?"

"Strawberry."

"Huh?" She reaches for the wine bottle and fills up her glass.

Michael sighs. "Whatever you want, Mom."

"Good, I was thinking vanilla too." She flops a big glob of icing on the cake. "Michael, don't you just love Frank Sinatra's music?"

"Yeah, whatever."

"I think everything you need to know about life is in Frank Sinatra's music."

Michael's never heard his mother talk about life before. The song ends on the radio and a commercial for laundry detergent comes on.

Michael turns off the radio and sits across from Vivian. "Mom, how're you doing, anyway?"

"Oh, wonderfully. The cake is going good." She spreads the icing with a little knife.

"Forget about the stupid cake. How are you doing? Really doing?"

Vivian blinks at Michael. "What in the world are you talking about?"

"I mean you and your life. How's it all going?"

"My life?" Vivian lets out a little laugh. "I really haven't thought that much about it. I guess my life is good."

"Why? Why haven't you thought about it?"

Vivian shrugs. "It's just not something we ever talked about. Too busy working and taking care of our families, I guess. When I was growing up, if we had a roof over our heads and food on the table, life was good."

"There has to be more to life than that."

Vivian spreads more icing over the cake. "My mother told me if I could marry a good man and support him in every way, be a good American, and be a loving mother, then that would be the greatest thing a woman could ever do."

"How's that working out?"

"Great, except for days I have to deal with the smart ass men in this family," Vivian says with a smile.

"Just remember where I got it from," laughs Michael.

"You didn't get it from my side of the family. You've always been like your father, Michael. Even when you were a little boy. On the other hand, Lenny is more like me."

"So why did you marry a smart ass guy like dad anyway?"

"I don't know why. All I know is that when I met your father, it was love at first sight."

Michael leans forward. "I didn't think love at first sight was real."

"Oh, it was real for me." Vivian sips from her wineglass. "I was at a USO dance. Your father walked up to me..." She looks out the window into the backyard where James is pruning yellow rose bushes and remembers a night back in 1943, a long time ago.

Chapter 18

Something in his Eyes

The large room of the Santa Monica USO Club glows from low lights and lit cigarettes. Duke Ellington's big band music plays while men in World War II uniforms swing pretty girls around.

Vivian sits alone at a table on the edge of the dance floor, sipping her soda. She is only eighteen and fresh off the farm in Kansas. Her white dress has a yellow rose pinned to it.

Twenty-one-year-old James Muller is in his army uniform. He leans against a wall surveying the scene. His eyes stop at the prettiest girl he's ever seen. Taking a deep breath, he walks over to Vivian's table.

The minute Vivian looks up at James, her arms fill with goose bumps.

"So tell me," says James, "why is the prettiest girl at this dance sitting here all alone with no one to dance with? Is your dance card full?"

"No Corporal," she says, "my dance card is not full. Maybe I'm more woman than most men can handle."

James grins. "Wow...sounds dangerous."

Vivian grins too. "Very."

"Okay, how about a test drive? How about a dance? I'm James Muller."

"Alright James, you look brave enough. I'm Vivian Russo."

"Oh, you're Italian, I'm a lucky guy."

"Yes, and you're a German. This could mean trouble."

James takes Vivian by the hand and pulls her close onto the dance floor. After a little while, he whispers in her ear. "This isn't so bad."

Vivian just smiles.

After a little while longer, James slides his hand down Vivian's back. Before she can stop him, he touches the top of her butt. Vivian slaps his face as hard as she can, stomps off the dance floor, and plops back into her chair.

People laugh. For a moment, James stands on the dance floor embarrassed and dazed. Then he walks to Vivian and gets down on his knees.

Vivian keeps her chin high and her head tilted away.

"Please," begs James. "Please, I'm so sorry."

Vivian turns and looks straight into James' tear-filled eyes.

Chapter 19

Pearls of Wisdom

Vivian turns her gaze from the kitchen window to Michael. "It was in that moment...I knew...this was the man I would marry."

"But how?" asks Michael. "How could you know that?"

"I really don't know how. All I know is there was something in his eyes."

"Besides tears?" Michael jokes.

"Yes, yes, besides tears. Looking in his blue eyes it was like...I already knew this man. Even though we had never met before that night."

"And, as they say, the rest is history."

"And someday the same thing's going to happen to you, Michael."

"Some girl is going to slap me?"

"Besides that, smart ass. I mean you'll look into some girl's eyes and you'll know right then, in that moment—"

"What will I know?"

"You'll know that there are other women out there. Women, who like myself, love a good-looking smart-ass guy. And this woman will be the love of your life and the only girl for you."

"Really? Any other pearls of wisdom for me?" Michael grins. "Anything that doesn't involve Frank Sinatra's music."

"Hmm. Wisdom for my son. Sure. This one sounds simple but isn't. Never judge a book by its cover."

Michael rolls his eyes. "That's the best you can do?"

"Think about it," says Vivian. "You would be surprised how much ground those words cover."

"Okay, okay. Anything else?"

"There are no such things as coincidences. Everything happens for a reason."

Michael laughs. "So, what's the reason you're telling me these things?"

"Very funny! I can tell you one more thing. The real reason why things happen to us is far more complicated than we'll ever know."

Michael presses his hands together, bows to Vivian, and says in a joking voice. "The wisdom of the ages. Thank you Mom."

Vivian puts her hands together, bows back to Michael, and speaks in a Chinese accent. "Now honorable son, you must tell your honorable father that dinner will be ready in twenty minutes."

Michael stands and bows again. "Yes, wise old mama-san." He swipes the icing with his fingers, puts his fingers in his mouth, and winks at Vivian.

Vivian gives him a playful frown as he heads out the back door.

Chapter 20

Dropping Bombs on Your Own Grandmother

James pops open a can of beer and lights up a cigarette. Then he leans back in his lawn chair to admire the rose bushes he just pruned.

James is now forty-nine years old. He is in middle management at a transmission parts company. He has two cars, two televisions, a dog and a cat. James could be a poster boy for what the average middle age American would look like in 1970 America. James has put on an extra fifty pounds. A wonderful testimony to Vivian's baking ability. His life is pretty boring now. The days had drifted into weeks, weeks had turned into months. Twenty years in the blink of an eye...gone.

His father, Rolf, had put on weight in middle age too. But James hoped the similarities ended there. Rolf was one of those pain in the asses that was right most the time. Very intelligent and he knew it. When he made his mind up on something there was no changing it. He really had a love hate relationship with him. His Dad was really funny sometimes but boy could he argue with someone.

Rolf was in the First World War, as a German solider. Rolf's best friend in the war was a German solider by the name of Eric Johanson. They were both from Munich. As teenage boys, they thought joining the army and seeking glory while saving the fatherland would be exciting. Those posters they pasted everywhere, sure made the war look like fun.

Four years of fun in the trenches of France and the boys thought very differently.

Unlike Eric, Rolf was a very learned man. Rolf would read almost every book he could get his hands on. In 1917 while he was having fun in the trenches of France, Rolf found a book on a dead English solider. This book would change Rolf's life forever. The book was James Joyce's *A Portrait of the Artist as a Young Man*. Rolf was very impressed with James Joyce as an author. So much so, that he named his first-born son after him, much to the dismay of his parents.

After the war, times were hard in Germany. Rolf married Sara and moved back to his parent's farm on the outskirts of Dresden.

Rolf's Uncle Joseph lived in America. Joseph was smart, or maybe he was lucky. Because he missed all the insanity of the First World War. He had been in the German Merchant Marines in the late 1890's.

Portland, Oregon was a boom town when Joseph got there. He found he could make twice the money he was making on the ship by working in the woods. So he jumped ship and went to the nearest lumber camp. He worked in the woods until he had saved enough money to start his own lumber company.

In 1920, he sent money over to Germany to give his nephew and wife a new start. A new start for them and since Joseph had no children, maybe someone to pass the business on to. Rolf and Sara moved to Portland, Oregon in 1921, a year before James was born.

James's parents were very proud of their German ancestry and made sure their two sons learned the German language as they were growing up. Life was good for James and his family in the Pacific Northwest. His father worked at his uncle's lumberyard as a foreman.

Even though there were some tough times in America after the First World War, it was nothing compared to what Germany would experience. By November 1923, the American dollar was worth 4,210,500,000,000 German marks. It took a wheelbarrow full of paper money just to buy a loaf of bread.

James took a swig of beer, thinking how strange his life was. If his folks hadn't moved to America in 1921, he could have just as easily been wearing a German uniform during the war instead of an American one.

For James the years in the Army were the happiest of his life. He closes his eyes, remembering that Sunday morning in December 1941, when it all began.

"Those dirty Japs bombed Pearl Harbor!" James announces as he marches into the kitchen. "I just heard it on the radio."

His mother, Sara, stops cooking and sinks into a chair. Rolf lowers his coffee cup on the table and puts his head in his hands. But James is excited. War is finally coming and James can't wait for the grand adventure. He stays glued to the radio the rest of the day listening to every report and later to Roosevelt's speech.

A few days later, James tells his father he plans to enlist. But Rolf tries to convince him to stay home, by telling him again of the horrors of war. "And you could end up killing other Germans, and maybe even your own relatives."

"That won't happen," James insists. "I'm requesting to be placed where I'll only be killing Japanese."

"Well," says Rolf, "at least they won't be our relatives."

Within weeks, James arrives at boot camp and takes to the army like a duck does to water. He loves the structure and discipline and camaraderie. He meets his best buddies there, Bob, George, and Stan.

One day, he's called to the commander's office. "I see from your file Private Muller," says the commander, "that you are of German ancestry and speak German. And your father was a German soldier in the last war, is this correct?"

"Yes sir, it is," says James standing tall at attention.

"So Private, do you have any problem killing Germans?"

"I'd rather not, sir. But I'll do whatever is necessary."

"Right now it's necessary to win this war and to do that we're going to need to kill lots of Germans...right?"

"Yes sir!"

"This army will need lots of German interpreters. What if we promoted you to a corporal? It pays twelve dollars more a month and you would become an interpreter for the US army. So Mr. Muller would you have a problem killing Germans now?"

"Not one bit sir. I'd be happy to do so."

"Good then. We have high hopes for you Corporal Muller. You're dismissed."

James leaves the captain's office with a big smile on his face. He thinks to himself "Hey...twelve bucks more a month and two chevrons instead of one, plus the Captain said he had high hopes for me too."

Back at home, James's dad has high hopes for James too—that his son won't be killing any of his friends or relatives. He thinks of his family and mother that are still back in Germany and wonders how this war might be affecting them too.

James is back in his barracks and flops on his bunk. He thinks about how strange life can be. He thinks, that the big difference with who you might end up killing in a war could be one small move. Just over a border and in a different country and twenty years later your kids could be dropping bombs on their own grandmother. But what's the odds of that? Besides he never even met his Grandmother and she probably a Nazis anyway.

C'est la guerre!

Chapter 21

The Talk

In the backyard, Michael crosses over to James who sits on a lawn chair staring into the rose bushes. Michael thinks of James squeezing Mom's butt at the USO dance and realizes he doesn't really know his father. There were camping trips and outings to the baseball park. But there had never been any real talks—except for the famous sex talk that lasted less than a minute.

Michael grits his teeth remembering when he was sixteen-years-old.

James is shaving in the bathroom as Michael walks by.

"Michael come in here for a minute." James never takes his eyes off the mirror. "Your mother wanted me to talk to you about uh....you know...sex."

"Oh," is all Michael can say.

"I'm sure you know how it all works. So I have only two things to say to you. Be careful, the last thing you want to do is get some young stupid girl knocked up...right?"

"Uh...that's right, Dad."

"Okay. The other thing I want to tell you is to always go after the good looking girls. They're just as lonely as the ugly ones! Got it?"

"Yeah, sure Dad."

"Make me proud son."

Now in the backyard, Michael shakes his head. That's his dad, always waiting for Michael to make him proud. He steps up to James. "Mom says dinner in twenty minutes."

James takes a drag from his cigarette. "Yeah... great...uh... have a seat. We need to talk."

"Okay, shoot," says Michael, pulling up a lawn chair. "What's on your mind?"

"Have you thought anymore about...you and the army?"

"Jesus, Dad, not this again!"

"Yes, this again! Goddamn it, you need to think about your future and doing your part to protect our freedom."

"Really? And just how is your freedom being affected by what's happening ten thousand miles away in Southeast Asia?"

"The problem son, is those people over there want to be communistic!"

"Yeah...so?"

"We need to stop them over there. Or they will be on our doorstep before you know it."

"If that's true, why don't we invade Cuba? They're communist and only ninety miles away from us."

"I'm telling you, the communists must be stopped. Not next week or year."

"Stop them? Just like you did with the Germans in World War II?"

"Goddamn it...that's right! Just like me and many others did in the war."

"But don't you care about the deaths? Didn't you even lose friends in the war?"

"Sure. We all did. I lost three of my closest friends in just one day. Bob, George, and Stan, three of the best guys you'd ever meet. The crazy thing is, the war was already technically over."

James gazes at the rose bushes again and remembers a day back in July 1945.

Chapter 22

Vino!...Vino!...Vino!

It's a hot summer day. James and his outfit are heading across France in a convoy of ten trucks heading to a French port. Then they'll be shipped out to God-knows-where.

The European war was over in May. But instead of going home, they'd been sent orders to get ready to invade Japan. They had escaped one hell just to be sent to another.

The trucks stop for lunch on the outskirts of a small French village. As James and his friends climb out of the trucks, a small group of Frenchmen approach. The Frenchmen put their fingers to their lips as if they were smoking. *Cigarettes...cigarettes... American cigarettes!*

The Americans smile and put their hands to their mouths as if they were drinking wine. *Vino... Vino...Vino!*

The Frenchmen turn on their heals and twenty minutes later return with a wooden box of wine bottles.

"Great," George said. "We're in business."

"Yeah," says Stan, "but are these guys going to charge us? James you speak any French?"

"No, just German. But don't worry, I'll get us a deal."

James pulls two packs of Lucky Strikes from his pocket and gives them to the oldest Frenchman.

Then he holds up two fingers in one hand and one finger in the other and smiles.

The Frenchman shakes his head and holds up five fingers.

James frowns and holds up three fingers.

The Frenchman gives James a dirty look and picks up the box and starts to turn around.

"Mother fuckers!" Bob says as he grabs his Thompson submachine gun. "These guys would be speaking German if wasn't for us."

"Come down Bob," says James, "your not going to shoot anybody."

"Okay, okay asshole," says James, grabbing the old Frenchman's arm. "I'm going to save your life." He puts his hand up with five fingers raised. The Frenchman puts the box down. "Come with me, you goddamn bandit and I'll get your smokes." They head toward the truck.

James calls out to Bob, George, and Stan. "Hey, I got this since I have more smokes than the rest of you put together."

Stan gives the old Frenchman the finger as he passes by. Then he grabs a wine bottle from the box with Bob and George.

James retrieves his duffel bag from the truck and reaches in for three cartons of cigarettes. He looks up and laughs at his friends struggling to get the corks out of their wine bottles. "Hey you guys, can't you even wait for me!"

George grins. "Better hurry before it's all gone."

"A toast to you guys," says Stan.

Bob clinks his bottle against George's. "To the end of this fucking war."

Stan nods his head. "And may we never see Japan."

All three men put the bottles to their mouths and take a big drink. George's eyes look ready to pop out of his head as he grabs his throat. Stan screams out. "What the hell!" He spits the white liquid mixed with blood out of his mouth.

Bob throws his bottle to the ground and cries through a choked voice. "These French assholes are trying to kill us!"

Chapter 23

The Business of War

James sighs in his lawn chair and lights another cigarette. "It was the saddest thing I ever saw," he says to Michael. "My friends rolling on the ground and dying and there was nothing I could do to help them."

"They all died?"

"George and Stan died in just a few minutes. We loaded Bob in the truck and drove like hell to Paris, but he died the next day."

"But why would the French want to kill you guys?"

"They didn't. It was all a big mistake. There was a big court case. They were all found innocent. Seems the French were making their own soap during the war. They were using lye and stored it old wine bottles. Somehow the bottles got mixed up and my friends paid the price with their lives."

"Wow."

"Crazy thing is we wouldn't drink the beer in Germany because we thought the Krauts would try and poison it. We used the beer bottles for target practice. Then to be poisoned by our own allies. To make it through the war and die like that."

"It makes no sense, but what does in war. Jim Morrison says that death makes angels of us all.'"

"Michael, I never told anyone this but the day after Bob died I drove back to that French village.

I was going to kill all those guys. When I got there, I found the old Frenchman's son. I thought about killing him too just to make him pay for what he had done. But after talking to him I knew these guys didn't want to kill us."

"Did you ever kill anyone up close?"

James nods. "It was in one of those him-or-me situations. This poor German bastard hesitated and I didn't. It's only by the grace of God that I'm sitting here today. He was as close as you are now."

Michael stays silent waiting to hear more.

"What was really crazy," says James, "was that since I was an interpreter for the army, I talked to him in German right before he died."

"What? No way! You talked to him after you shot him?"

"I think he knew it was nothing personal. It was...more like just what happens in the business of war."

"Business of war? What could be more personal than killing someone?"

James takes a drag from his cigarette and slowly blows out some smoke. "Well, he must have trusted me."

"Why?"

"Before he died, he gave me a photo of his mother and sister."

Michael's mouth drops open. "This dying German guy gave you a photo of his family?"

"Yes."

"Why would he do that?"

James shrugs. "I don't know. Guess he wanted

me to contact them after the war and tell them what happened to their son."

"Did you?"

"Are you out of your mind? Me contact them? What would I've said? Hi. I'm James Muller. You don't know me. I'm the guy that killed your son in the war. So how are you all doing?"

"That's sick!"

James rubs his cigarette out on his chair, then flicks the butt into the rose bushes. "Believe it or not, I think I still have that photo somewhere, maybe in my army album."

"Maybe you should have taken a photo of all the people you killed in the war and put them in your army album too."

"God damn it! I knew I should never have told you about what happened."

"You call it the business of war? I call it killing people. But maybe you're right. Maybe it is the business of war, because it seems that the soldiers of today are no more than the security guards for America's corporations anyway."

"We must do what our country tells us to do. What good is a man without his country?"

"What if believing in your country costs you one of the most precious things in your life?"

"And what is that Michael?"

"Me!"

"So that's it. My son is a coward!"

"Coward? If you want to die and kill for your country...great. But you can count me out."

"What if everyone one felt that way, Michael? What then?"

"Are you serious? If everyone felt like me, there would be no more wars."

"Goddamn it! You know what I'm talking about."

"As long as people like you think killing for your governments and your churches is the only way to bring peace and security, we are all in big trouble."

"I know God is with America."

"Oh, really Dad? Just America? Don't you think everyone would like to believe that God loves only his country? What kind of god would just love one country or even favor half a dozen countries. Do you know how stupid that sounds?"

"Yes but—"

"The parents of this planet have no problem killing their children and other people's children for their ideals. No Dad, you're not offering up this son to the gods of war! And by the way Dad, shame on you for even asking."

"Dinner is ready!" Vivian's voice rings out from the back door.

Michael stands. "Tell mom I'm not hungry. I don't want to eat with someone who is trying to kill me."

James jumps out of his chair, knocking it over. "God damn it Michael...sometimes you make me so angry I think I could..."

"Sometime it feels like you already have."

Chapter 24

Catch 22

Michael's car has two bumper stickers. One is a peace sign, the other says, "Please God Protect Me From Your People." He hops in his car, spins out of the driveway, and speeds off into the sunset. Jim Morrison's voice booms from the tape deck, this time singing the song "People are Strange."

Within minutes, Michael reaches Susan's neatly trimmed house and strides up the walkway. He looks over at all the toy guns scattered across grass.

A middle-aged woman answers the door with a smirk.

"Good evening Mrs. Weber," says Michael. "Is Susan around?"

"I'm sure she is. Come in. I'll get her. Wait in the living room. Bill! Michael's here."

Bill sits in an overstuffed chair watching the 6:00 news. "Hey Michael, check this out." He shakes his head in disbelief, pointing to the TV. The screen shows a Buddhist monk dousing himself with gasoline and setting himself on fire. "Why in the hell would anyone do that?"

"I guess he feels strongly against the war," says Michael.

"What a stupid son of a bitch."

The next scene shows B-52 bombers dropping high explosives on their target. Bill smiles.

"That's what they should do. They need to bomb those guys back into the Stone Age. If it was up to me and if I had anything to say about it, I would even use the big one. Nuke them all."

Michael stares at Bill. "You mean the A bomb?"

"Sure, why not? It ended the last war didn't it?"

"Who knows? Maybe they don't want to end it. It's been going on for seven years with no end in sight."

Bill gives Michael a confused look. "Why on Earth would anyone want to prolong the war?"

"Maybe it's good for business. Don't you work for Hughes Helicopter?"

"Yeah...so?"

"Where would you be if the war ended tomorrow?"

"Uh... well...I..."

Susan, a tall good-looking blond bounces into the living room with bright, happy eyes. "Michael! I haven't seen you in weeks."

"Want to go to a movie?"

"Sure! I'll get my sweater." She hurries out of the room.

"I'd have no problem getting another job, Michael," says Bill.

Back on the TV, Walter Cronkite announces the good news. "A big day yesterday in Southeast Asia, the body count is 1246 NVA and Viet Con dead and just 66 Americans dead and missing."

"I wonder what the body count would be Mr. Weber if they dropped the big one," says Michael.

Susan sashays into the room with a pink cashmere sweater under her arm and grabs Michael by the hand. "Bye, Dad."

"You be back by midnight, young lady."

"Sure, Dad."

Susan squeezes Michael's arm as they walk to the car. "It's so good to see you."

"Huh? Oh. Yeah."

"So, my love, where are we heading?" asks Susan.

Michael starts the car. "I thought we'd hit a drive-in movie."

"Sounds fun. What's playing?"

"You'll love it. It's kind of a war movie, called Catch 22. I read the book in high school."

"Another war movie," says Susan sounding disappointed. "Well, okay. As long as I'm with you, I'll watch anything."

They drive a few miles with the top down passing rows of orange groves. One of the giant sprinklers dumps a bunch of water into the open car. They both laugh.

Michael glances over at this gorgeous woman sitting next to him in her wet white blouse. It's very evident she's not wearing a bra. He knows that guys would kill to be with her—she was perfect in every way. But something was missing for him and he had no idea what. He thought back to what his mother said about love at first sight. He never felt that spark with Susan, or any other girl. A pang of guilt hits Michael. He knows Susan's in love with him. And he's nowhere near in love with her.

They pick up some hamburgers and fries at McDonalds and park under the shade of a large eucalyptus tree.

Michael eats silently, staring out the windshield.

"What's wrong, Michael?"

"I don't know, nothing and everything." He swallows a bite. "I got into it again with my father about the war. He has no respect for how I feel...If I'm drafted and don't go into the army, they'll put me in prison. It's kill or go to jail. I don't want to do either. I promise you Susan, I will not go to war."

"But what can you do if it's the law?"

"I don't know, maybe go to Canada."

"You feel that strongly about it?"

"Two guys from my high school came back from Viet Nam and killed themselves. What could they have done or seen that made them do that? There's only one person I can stop from going to war. And that's me." Michael tosses his half-eaten hamburger into the bag and starts up the engine. "Let's get the hell out of here."

At the drive-in, Michael parks the car in the back row. Then he gets a couple of beers from the cooler in the trunk and hands one to Susan. The movie begins flashing on the screen. Michael hangs the speaker on the window and leans back, eager to watch. Susan tries to snuggle next to him, but Michael just crosses his arms.

After the scene where Lieutenant Nately and the Old Man talk about morals, Michael turns to Susan. "That says it all. It's what I'm talking about. My life is a huge catch 22. People say war is insane but I'm called the crazy one because I don't want to go to war. I mean what could be more crazy?"

"Can't you just leave it alone, Michael?"

Michael's back straightens. Susan, he realizes, is like all the others in his life, wishing he'd just conform to the status quo. "You're not really interested in this movie are you?" he asks.

"No, not really."

Michael unhooks the speaker and starts up the car. They drive to Susan's house in silence. When they get there, Michael parks on the street and turns off the engine. "I really like you, Susan."

"Do you Michael?"

"Yes I do."

"But."

"But, I can't do this anymore," says Michael.

"You can't do what anymore?"

"Lead you on. I really enjoy your company but there something that's just not right between us."

"Oh really?" says Susan. "Well I'll tell you what's not right. You are a jerk for one. All these months I've been here for you. Weeks go by and you don't even call. You've treated me like dirt. I hate you and all your whining about the war shit. You know, Michael, this is the greatest country on Earth, and why out of all the guys I could have picked, I picked the one guy who I'm embarrassed to bring home to my parents. My parents know about you."

"What do they know about me?"

"Forget it, I'm done." Susan opens up the car door and gets out. She glares at Michael. "I hope some woman breaks your heart the way you've broken mine."

"I'm really sorry I hurt you."

"Well I hate you Michael, please just get out of here." She storms up the walkway and disappears into the house.

As Michael drives away, he can't help but think how strange love is. How people "fall" in love. How people "fall" out of love. How love can turn on a dime and become hatred almost instantly.

Deep in his bones, Michael knows he's experienced all of it—love, hate, betrayal—before. But how can that be? He's never even been in love.

He thinks of Susan storming up the walkway and smiles. He could have asked her to marry him instead of dumping her. What would have happened then? Maybe, just maybe, he did her the biggest favor of her life.

They would have gotten married, had two kids. Then years later, she'd realize she married someone who wasn't really in love with her. She'd have felt really betrayed then.

"Yep, one day she'll be thanking me," he says to himself, "but not any time soon."

Chapter 25

Mehr Sein Als Schenen

An empty beer can falls to the ground as Michael stumbles out of his car. He shuffles around to the back of the house and into the kitchen, hoping to avoid his parents.

James and Vivian sit on the couch staring at the TV. They're watching "Laugh In." A German soldier on the show says, "Veeeery interesting... veeeery interesting, but stupid!" James and Vivan laugh. They don't notice Michael as he slips past them and up the staircase.

When Michael reaches his bedroom, his hand grips the doorknob. But then he stops. He turns and walks up one more flight of stairs and into the attic. Michael pulls on an old string hanging from the ceiling, and a bare light bulb switches on. He steps over boxes of junk and around old furniture. When he locates the old trunk, he opens it up. His father's old army uniform lies on top.

Michael digs into the trunk until he finds his father's army album. Then he settles down under the pool of light. Turning the pages, he sees photos of his father in basic training, and photos of his parents dancing at the USO club. "He's wasn't much older than I am now," Michael mutters.

On another page, Michael sees a photo of his father's three army buddies. Could they be George, Stan, and Bob—the same guys that died in

France? Michael flips the page and the hair on his arms stands up. It's the photo of Mary and Leni. He lifts the photo off the album page. Old dried blood is smeared along the edges. Michael turns the photo over to see an address and some German writing.

Something keeps Michael from putting the photo back. Instead, he slips the photo into his shirt pocket. When he returns the album to the trunk, a shiny object at the bottom catches his eye. An SS dagger. He takes the knife out of the sheath. On the blade is the inscription "Mehr Sein Als Schenen." Michael has no idea what the words mean. But he knows he's holding an instrument of death. Why did my Dad have this? Michael wonders. Did he get it from the dead German his father had told him about? Michael stuffs the knife back in the trunk and heads down the stairs to his bedroom.

Michael's bedroom has two travel posters hanging on the wall: one of France and the other of Germany. World War II model airplanes hang from the ceiling. He retrieves an English-German dictionary from the bookshelf and takes the photo out of his pocket. It takes him a while, but he finally translates the words on the back: "For my Michael. Come home safely. This is my new address. I'll wait for you there. Love, Mary." Michael has a lump in his throat. Could this woman still be alive?

Michael looks up the words that were on the SS dagger. "Mehr Sein Als Schenen." He speaks the words out loud, "Be More Than You Appear To Be." Then he flops on the bed and laughs. "What does that mean? Be more Nazi than you look like?"

Lenny opens the bedroom door. "Hey, what did you say to Dad to get him so worked up today?" asks Lenny.

"Why, what'd he say?"

"He was waving the flag around at the dinner table again. He said you weren't a good American. That you didn't want to help your country when it really needs you and—"

"I won't help my country do what? Go to Vietnam and kill people, so they don't become communistic? Wouldn't it be funny, if they all ended up being communist anyway, whether anyone fought there or not?"

"That'll never happen. America's never lost a war."

"There's a first time for everything." Michael picks up the photo again.

"What are you looking at?" asks Lenny.

"Nothing."

Lenny swipes the photo out of Michael's hand. "Let's have a look."

"Be careful, that photo is over thirty years old."

"Who are these people?" asks Lenny.

"Dad killed the woman's son in the war."

"What? No way!"

"Yep. Dad told me the whole story today in the backyard."

"Wow...creepy!"

"What's creepy is there's something about that photo. It's weird, those two people..."

"Yeah, there's something about their eyes. The girl is—"

"Old enough to be your mother. I'm sure they're probably both dead by now."

"Wouldn't it be crazy if they 're both still living?"

"Real crazy."

The phone rings in the upstairs hall. Vivian's voice calls from the kitchen. "It's Kirk on the line for Michael."

"I got it Mom," announces Lenny.

Kirk's voice jumps through the line. "Michael"?"

"No, it's Lenny."

"Put your brother on the line, Lenny. I've got some really good news for you both."

Lenny hands the phone to Michael.

"Yeah, what's up?"

"Michael, you're not going to believe it but the stars are in alignment. We, my friend, are going to Germany, to Oktoberfest!"

"What're you talking about?"

"I'm talking about the three of us, you, me, and Lenny, going to the biggest beer festival in the world, in Munich. Remember Germany, the place you've always wanted to visit?"

"Yeah."

"I told you about my aunt who lives in Munich. She's going to Italy for three weeks in September and said we're welcome to stay at her place for free."

"Kirk you are—"

"I know. A God!"

"No. You are crazy. There's no way I can go. School is starting in September. Plus there's my job. There's no way they would let me take off for three weeks. I'm really sorry but I'm going to have to pass on this one."

"You're turning your back on a trip of a lifetime?"

"Yep...I guess I am."

"Michael, you're half German and half Italian, right?

"Yeah, so?"

"So I'm going to talk to your Italian side now. You... Michael...need...to go on this trip. If you don't, you'll regret it the rest of your life."

"Nein, nien, nien!"

"Michael, you have concrete for brains," says Kirk. "Do me a favor and put your brother on."

Michael hands the phone to Lenny who has been standing there listening the whole time. Back in his bedroom, Michael sits in a chair, pulling on his eyebrows as he stares at the German travel poster on the wall.

Lenny pops his head in. "Kirk wanted me to talk some sense into you. He has it all figured out. It'd cost us an airline ticket and maybe a few hundred bucks a piece for the whole trip. You can get away with missing a few weeks of school. So you just have to get off from your job."

Michael chews on his lip.

"At least sleep on it," says Lenny. "Because, I won't go unless you do."

After Lenny leaves, Michael takes his pants and shirt off and throws them over a chair. He picks up the photo again. "So, girls, what do you say?" Then he sets the photo down on his night stand, turns out the light, and goes to sleep.

Michael, in a World War II German uniform, heads down a street. People seem to know him. An old man points his finger at Michael and laughs. Michael walks to a house where there's a cat on the windowsill. Inside the house, he sees Mary sitting at the kitchen table looking at photos spread out before her.

Michael comes closer, but her eyes stay fixed on the photos.

"Mary?" asks Michael.

"Yes. Michael is it you?"

"It's me."

"What took you so long?"

"I got here as fast as I could. Is it too late?"

"Michael, you know it's never too late."

"What are you doing here?" asks Michael.

"Waiting."

"Waiting? For what?"

Mary finally looks up at Michael. "Waiting to go home of course. Everyone is gone now and I want to go home too. I have just one thing left to do, before I can go." *Mary turns her gaze back to the photos.*

"Where are you now?" asks Michael. "Where is this place?"

"You know where it is."

"I don't. Where is Leni?"

"You know where she is," says Mary. "Oh, Michael don't forget."

"Don't forget what?"

"The flowers, of course."

"What flowers?" asks Michael.

"You know, the yellow roses. Oh...by the way, someone is here for you." *The door flies open and*

Michael turns around to see his father James in an American uniform pointing a rifle at him.

The clock radio punches on with Frank Sinatra's song, "My Way." Michael startles awake. "Wow. What was that all about?"

The phone rings. Vivian's voice echoes up the stairs. "Michael! It's for you."

Michael pulls his pants on and picks up the phone in the hall. "Hello...yeah what's going on, Bob? What...are you kidding me? Really? The whole shop... two months? Yeah...gee okay...I guess I'll be by to pick up my check tomorrow...yeah see ya."

Michael shakes his head as he hangs up the phone, then heads downstairs to the kitchen. Vivian has made him a breakfast of scrambled eggs and toast.

"Mom, you'll never believe it. There was a fire at the shop last night. They're closing the shop to make repairs."

"What're you going to do?" asks Vivian.

Michael looks out the kitchen window at the yellow rose bushes. "I don't know. But I can tell you one thing. The last twenty four hours has been some of the craziest in my life."

"A lot can happen in one day."

"It's almost like...I have no choice now...but to..."

"What?" asks Vivian.

"Go to Germany, I guess."

"Germany? I don't think so!"

Chapter 26

Only Two Options

At the Los Angeles International Airport, Michael, Kirk and Lenny reach their gate just as the flight is boarding. Kirk grins at Michael. "Hey man, I'm glad your Italian side won out this time."

"It took us two weeks of fighting with our parents to make this happen," says Lenny. "But it'll be worth it."

Kirk winks at the airline attendant taking their tickets. Michael doesn't remember, but she is the same woman who was the German waitress in the restaurant called The Three Roses in his past life.

Lenny grabs the window seat and Kirk takes the aisle. Michael settles in the middle. "I don't know," he says. "I have this strange feeling this could be the biggest mistake of my life."

"Jesus, Michael," says Kirk, "will you give it up—all this doom and gloom? I'm going to remind you of this when you're drunk on your ass with some foxy German babe hanging on your arm."

Michael smiles. "You're right. Even though I'm going to Germany. It's time to let my Italian side out."

"Hey, La vita viva all'il più Pieno."

Hours later, they arrive at JFK Airport in New York for a two hour layover. As the plane makes its way to the gate, Michael leans over to Lenny. "I have a surprise for you," he says. "We're going to see Grandpa Joe. I found his phone number in Mom's address book. He's meeting us here in the airport."

"That crazy old man? Mom hates his guts."

"I'm sure he has a story to tell and I, for one, want to hear it. He's our grandfather and we really don't know a thing about him."

"We know he's a gangster."

"Huh?" asks Kirk. "A gangster?"

"Yeah," says Michael. "He's in the family, if you know what I mean."

"The family?"

"The family...Costa Nostra...you know, the Mafia."

"No way!" says Kirk.

When Michael, Kirk, and Lenny walk through the gate, an old man shuffles over. He looks too thin for his well-pressed suit and the lines in his face are deep.

"Grandpa Joe?" asks Michael.

Joe stands there for a moment staring at his two grandsons who are now such fine young men. He'd only seen them once before, and he can't help but think about his thirty-one years in prison. How they robbed him of so many things, like seeing his grandsons growing up. He reaches out his arms. "Come on and give your old grandpa a hug!"

Michael and Lenny embrace Joe. Then Michael motions for Kirk to come close. "Kirk, this is Joe Ruso. Grandpa, this is our friend Kirk."

"Good to meet you, Kirk," says Joe. He pats Michael's cheek and then Lenny's. "God, I've missed you guys. Let's go have a beer."

They find a small cafe in the airport and sit down. "Four beers please...Rheingold," Joe says to the waitress. After she returns with the beers, Joe speaks to Kirk. "Would you mind if I had a few minutes with my boys alone?"

"Not at all, Mr. Ruso." Kirk grabs his beer and walks off.

"So," says Joe, "you boys are going to Germany. Sounds like fun."

"Yeah," says Michael, "want to come along?"

"Sure," says Joe with a grin, "but I don't think you boys could keep up with me." He takes a swig of beer. "I'm really glad to see you both. You're my favorite grandsons."

"We're your *only* grandsons," says Lenny.

"Yes...I know."

"Well," says Michael, "you're our only Italian grandfather."

"Yes, I am. In this life, boys, you have only two options. You can either be an Italian or be with an Italian—other than that you're screwed."

"But we are only half Italian," says Michael.

"I'm going to overlook that! Say, why are you boys going to Germany anyway? Italy is a much nicer place."

"It's a long story," says Lenny.

"We don't have time for long stories, do we now? There is something I need to give you." Joe takes two white envelopes from his coat pocket and puts them on the table in front of the boys. "A little something for your trip."

Michael looks inside one of the envelopes. "Grandpa, you're too generous."

"Nonsense. I feel bad that I haven't done more for you both." Joe gets the crazy feeling that he may never see his two grandsons again, and anger rises in his throat at all the lost time. "That crazy bitch, your grandmother, drove a stake in my heart when she took Vivian to California before the war."

"What happened between you two anyway?" asks Michael, leaning forward.

"That's none of our business," says Lenny.

"No, no. I'll tell you," says Joe. "I need to tell you." He stares into his beer while the story pours out.

Chapter 27

What Could be Crueler?

It is 1931. His wife Maria comes home, her cheeks flushed. "I'm leaving you," she says.

Joe shuts his eyes tight. He knew this day would come. He'd fallen in love with Maria the second he saw her all those years ago. But she was always in love with his best friend, Carmine, who was married to Rose. Now Rose had died and Maria and Carmine were free to be together.

"And I'm taking Vivian," says Maria.

"But she's only five," says Joe. "She'll miss her dad."

"You can visit her."

Maria packs her bags that night, and before Joe knows it, he's all alone, without his wife or daughter.

Maria and Carmine marry and move in with Carmine's father who needs some help getting around. They live just three blocks away. Joe is the laughing stock of the neighborhood. He hates them both. To make matters worse, they only let Joe see Vivian every now and then.

When Vivian is six years old, Maria and Carmine go away on vacation. So Joe finally gets to have Vivian stay overnight. During her stay, she complains about itching and pain high up between her legs.

Joe asks his mother to check it out. Then he waits at the dining room table thinking how messed up his life is. He knew Maria didn't love him when they got married. He knew he was just a rebound for her. When Carmine married Rose, she had no choice but to marry Joe. What could be crueler than to marry someone you don't even love?

His mother comes in and puts her hand on Joe's shoulder. "I've looked at Vivian," she says. "Something is not right down there."

Joe and his mother take Vivian to the doctor the next day. After the exam, the doctor speaks to Joe alone. "Vivian has been sexually abused."

"Jesus Christ!" cries Joe. "Someone's messing with my little girl?"

"You must find out who it is," says the doctor, "and keep him away from her."

Joe and his mother grill Vivian for hours, but she says nothing. But Joe knows it has to be Carmine. Full of rage, Joe plots his revenge.

The first Sunday after Maria and Carmine return from vacation, Joe waits until Vivian and her mother go to church. Then he pulls the gun from his coat pocket and rings the doorbell.

Carmine opens the door.

"Joe, what the…?"

Chapter 28

Something Worse than Death

Joe looks up from his beer and into the stunned eyes of Lenny and Michael. "I couldn't let him live. I had to protect Vivian."

"You mean you killed him?" asks Michael.

"I did more than that. I tortured the son of a bitch. He denied it the whole time and insisted he didn't do it. In the end he begged for death. He knew what he had done."

"But Grandpa," says Michael, "that's the worst thing that anyone can do—take another's life."

"If only that was true." Joe grabs both the boy's hands. "Carmine was my best friend for Christ sake. We grew up together. He stole my wife and then he took my daughter's purity. He made me look like a fool in the neighborhood. No, you're wrong, betrayal is far worse than death. I know because I've been in hell for forty years. Looking back at my life, death would have been a blessing back then."

"Mom never told us," says Michael.

"She never knew," says Joe.

"All she told us is that you were a bad man because you were in the Mafia," says Lenny.

"Mafia?" says Joe. "I wish!"

"What happened after you killed him?" asks Lenny.

"I was caught and tried. Spent thirty-one years in prison. Your grandmother never told your mother the truth. She wouldn't believe Carmine did those things to Vivian. So she told her that her father was a gangster and was put in jail for murder. Then she took Vivian as far away from me as she could. They ended up in California."

"Wow, what a story," says Lenny.

Joe shakes his head. "Funny...how life works out. If I hadn't killed Carmine, Vivian would have never moved to California and met your father. She probably would have married an Italian boy from the Bronx and you boys would have never happened."

Michael starts to smile. "So I guess we should thank you for killing Carmine and—"

"It's not funny, Michael," says Lenny. He turns to Joe. "Mom thinks you killed some random person and that you're a terrible monster. She doesn't know you spent thirty-one years in prison to protect her."

"Yeah," says Michael. "That's not right."

"Maybe not," says Joe, "maybe we'll figure it out in heaven one day. The good news is I know I won't see that bastard Carmine up there, he'll be burning in hell."

"We need to tell Mom the truth about you," says Michael.

"No, don't. It'd just cause her more suffering. No need to dredge up the past with her. Promise me, you won't say a word."

"But Grandpa—"

"There are no buts about it! I want you both to promise me right now."

"Okay, okay," says Michael, "we promise."

"Lenny, you promise too?"

"Yes, Grandpa."

"Good! A toast to us la familia." Joe raises his beer and they all clink their glasses.

Joe spots Kirk sitting at a table at the other end of the cafe and waves him over. "Thank you Kirk for giving me some time with my boys. We had important family business to discuss."

"No problem, Mr. Ruso."

"The boys want a hit done and we were just discussing the details."

Kirk's eyes look ready to pop of their sockets.

Michael and Lenny laugh so loudly that everyone in the cafe stares.

Chapter 29

La Familia

By the time Joe says goodbye to his grandsons, he's exhausted. He trudges out of the airport terminal and heads towards his car, which is parked at the far end of the parking lot. It's the hottest September day he can ever remember.

He huffs and puffs all the way to his car, and his hands shake as he gets the keys out of his pocket and opens the car door. "Son of a bitch," he mutters, plopping onto the car seat. He wipes the sweat off his forehead, starts the car up, and puts the AC on full blast.

Still shaking, Joe sits there trying to catch his breath. He reaches into his pocket and pulls out his wallet. There he finds a faded picture of Vivian and Maria, when Vivian was only five years old. He stares at it for a minute and then looks out his car windshield as he hears the roar of a 747 climbing its way out of the heat.

The moment Joe looks back down at the picture, he feels something hit his chest like a sledgehammer. Joe thinks someone has shot him. He looks down at his chest, but sees no blood. Before his mind can register what is happening the sledgehammer hits again. Everything goes black.

Joe gazes down at the roof of his 1958 Chrysler. He is absolutely spell bound as he floats over the parking lot and into the sky above Kennedy airport. Jets are landing and taking off all around him. Soon he's moving faster than a 747, heading out of New York and into outer space. A complete calm engulfs him as he aims towards a bright light.

Joe stands on a dirt road on the outskirts of a small Italian village. As he walks towards the town, he realizes this is the birthplace of his parents. He was there only once, as a small child, but he never forgot it. When he reaches the village, he continues down a narrow street. His senses are sharpened. Smells and sights are overwhelming. He can't ever remember a time when he felt so euphoric, so alive.

Although Joe hasn't seen anyone yet, he hears distant voices and laughter. He walks towards the voices while his mind races. He knows he's dreaming, that he's just taking a nap on the front seat of his Chrysler. But he's never had a dream that felt so real before. If it is a dream, he thinks, I hope I never wake up.

Finally the narrow street opens up to a grand plaza. It looks like a huge wedding feast with tables laden with fruit and cheese and wine. Flowers are everywhere. But Joe doesn't see a bride or groom.

He steps further into the plaza and can't believe his eyes. There sitting next to the fountain is his mom and dad. They look so young and in love. He looks around and is surprised to see all his family and friends that have died years before. They all stand up and applaud him.

Joe gets goose bumps when he turns to see his Maria standing there, blowing him a kiss. As he walks toward her, someone taps him on the shoulder. He turns around and before he can say anything, a man is giving him a giant bear hug. Joe takes one step back to see who it is, and his mouth drops open. He's looking right into Carmine's smiling face.

"Welcome home, Joe, my friend. I told you I didn't do it!"

Chapter 30

George Patton

Three thousand miles over the Atlantic Ocean, Lenny peers out his small window at the fading light over the water. They're heading towards Germany, towards the unknown, and he has a feeling that this trip will change his life forever.

The interior lights are turned down low now that the movie "Patton" with George C. Scott is over. Kirk is fast asleep, as are most the other passengers on the plane. Michael has his nose in a book. "What's your book about?" asks Lenny in a low voice.

"Germany in World War II."

"You're a funny guy," says Lenny. "You're against the war and fighting. But ever since we were kids, you've had this strange fascination with the last world war."

"I know. It's weird. I don't know why." Michael closes his book. "So what's your book about?"

Lenny hands the book to Michael who reads the title out loud, "The Persistent Illusion."

"It's really interesting," says Lenny. "I like it. It's a love story about, you know...past lives. How maybe after we die, we come back again as different people."

"Why in hell would anyone ever do that?"

"I don't know. It says that before we incarnate we get together with our soul mates in heaven. We sit around with our friends and make plans about what we want to do for each other. We form agreements and contracts. You know, like who we'll marry and who our kids will be. Pretty crazy, huh?"

"Crazy? How about absolutely nuts! What else does it say?"

"Sometimes people will visit a place they've never been to before. But they feel like they know it like the back of their hand."

"You mean like a déjà vu?"

"Yeah. The book says that means they've been there before...in a past life."

"Very weird."

"It also says sometimes we meet people that are total strangers, but somehow we feel we've known them our whole lives. That they are actually old friends from past lives. It also talks about god bumps."

"What in the hell are those?"

"Most people call them goose bumps. You know, it's when the hair on your arms stands up. The bumps mean you're speaking a truth—a truth you might have forgotten. Or sometimes the bumps are telling us to remember something very important."

"Sounds like the biggest bunch of horse crap I've ever heard. Besides, what good is it to come back if you couldn't remember who you were in a past life?"

Lenny shrugs.

"None of the church leaders and really smart people believes in any of that crap," says Michael.

"I guess you're right, pretty strange ideas."

"Of course I'm right. Have I ever been wrong?

Let's get some sleep." Michael smiles to himself as he moves his pillow under his neck.

Lenny starts to close his eyes, then opens them. "Say, Michael, do you think General Patton was an idiot?"

"No...why?

"Because he believed in reincarnation."

"Really?"

"Yep. Good night. See you in Germany."

Chapter 31

The Fatherland

All the way in the taxi ride from the airport, Lenny and Kirk point out cathedrals and towers as the sites fly by. Michael can't stop smiling. He's finally in the city he's always dreamt of—Munich.

The taxi stops at Kirk's aunt's house. It's a classic two-hundred-year-old Bavarian home. Michael, Lenny, and Kirk climb out, then Kirk pulls a wad of German money from his pocket with a confused look. The cab driver picks through the bills and takes out the exact fair. Kirk gives him ten more German marks. "Bittle...danke schoen!"

The cab driver smiles and drives off.

"God, I love these people," says Kirk.

"God, I love this place," says Michael.

"I think I've died and gone to heaven," says Kirk.

"Me too," says Lenny.

They lug their bags into the house. Old wood panels line the walls, and in the living room is a huge stone fireplace. There's no fire burning, but the faint scent of smoke fills the house.

"Kirk, you are a god," says Michael. "Thank you for talking me into this."

"Talk you into this?" says Kirk. "I didn't talk you into anything. We've been wanting to make this trip to Germany ever since we were kids."

"You're right," says Michael, "but I didn't think we'd actually do it."

"Hey Michael, be careful what you wish for—"

"Yeah," says Lenny. "You just might get it!"

The second those words leave Lenny's mouth, Michael gets the chills. He looks down at his arms and sees goose bumps.

"I'm going to get settled in," Kirk announces. "Oh by the way, I get the master bedroom."

"Fine with us," says Lenny. "Then lets hit the bar we saw at the end of the street."

Kirk nods. "Sounds like a plan. I can't wait to get my hands on some of Germany's finest."

"Beer or women?" asks Lenny.

"Both! I hope."

Michael walks upstairs. "You guys go have a good time. I'm beat. I'm going to take a short nap. Maybe I'll catch up with you later."

"Suit yourself," says Kirk. "Hope to see you down there."

"Stay out of trouble," says Michael. "I'd recommend not bringing up the whole Nazi thing, to any of the locals around here. Even though it's been thirty years, they're still pretty sensitive to all that Hitler stuff."

Lenny and Kirk click their heels together and give Michael the German salute. "Seig Heil!" says Kirk.

"Seig heil...mein fuhrer!" says Lenny.

Lenny and Kirk start laughing. Michael waves them away with his hand. He finds his bedroom, closes the door behind him, and drops his bags. Then he lies on top of the bed and gazes at a photo on the wall of woman and small child. He shuts his eyes.

Michael climbs off the bed and turns on the light. The bedroom looks different than before. German voices echo from downstairs. Michael steps down the staircase. It's dark except for the glowing light from the fire in the fireplace. A young man and woman stand with their backs to Michael, warming their hands by the fire. The woman is wearing a long white dress.

As Michael steps closer, the man turns around. It is Michael's own smiling face reflecting back at him.

Michael wakes up in a fright and scans the room. When his breathing returns to normal, he walks out of his bedroom and down the hallway. Through Kirk's open door, Michael can see Kirk is asleep with all his clothes on. Kirk has red lipstick on his cheek and a big smile on his face. Michael walks further down the hallway to Lenny's bedroom and cracks open the door. Lenny is asleep too. Michael blinks in surprise. Sleeping next to Lenny is another man. "Oh my God," mutters Michael. "This is going to be one crazy trip."

Michael peers at the man and has a strange feeling. He doesn't remember, but the other man in Lenny's bed is one of the American soldiers Michael killed in World War II.

Downstairs in the kitchen, Michael finds a piece of paper and a pen. He scribbles a note and puts it on the refrigerator door, then leaves the house.

Chapter 32

Michael Finds his Women

It's a beautiful September morning filled with blue skies and autumn leaves. Michael wanders down the street not knowing where he's going. He finds himself in a park. Again, Michael doesn't remember, but this is the same park that he and Kristin were in before World War II. A rose bush catches his attention just as he hears a child's laughter. He turns to see a young woman sitting on a park bench with a small child. It's the same French woman and child that Michael found dead in World War II. Michael and the woman look at each other for a moment and smile.

Michael continues to wander. He walks out of the park and comes to a street corner. He looks up at the street sign.

"If I go down this street, I will come to a church in three blocks," Michael tells himself. He turns left and walks exactly three blocks. And there is it—the large church. He gets the chills. "How in the hell did I know a church would be right here?"

In front of the church, there are two taxis parked. Michael walks over to one of the taxis and pulls out the faded photo of Mary and Leni from his pocket. He hands the photo to the cab driver. The driver looks at the photo and opens his hands in a confused gesture. Michael turns the photo over and points to the address on its back. "Bitte...bitte."

The driver opens the car door and Michael climbs in. A few minutes later they are driving through the rundown part of the city. When the taxi pulls up in front of a rundown apartment building, the driver points to it. Michael checks the address on the back of the photo and it is the same address that is on the building. He draws a book out of his pocket. Turning the pages he finally finds what he is looking for. "Warte ein moment...bitte!"

The taxi driver nods his head.

Michael walks into the apartment building and up the stairs to the second floor. He checks the apartment number of the first apartment to his right. Then he swallows and rings the bell. A woman in her forties comes to the door. Michael knows this is not Mary by her age. He hands the photo to the woman and points to Mary. "Mary. Do you know this woman? Did a Mary live here?"

The woman frowns at the photo. Michael turns the photo over and points to the address.

"No... no," says the woman.

"Bitte!" Michael pleads.

The woman shakes her head and speaks in German. "No, I tell you I don't know this woman at all."

Michael curses under his breath. He has no idea what she's saying. "Bitte!" he says again. But she waves him off and shuts the door.

Halfway down the staircase, Michael hears the woman open her door and walk across the hallway. Then she knocks on a neighbor's door. An old woman in her eighties answers.

"Gertrude, do you know of a Mary that might have lived in my apartment at one time?"

"Yes, I know Mary. Why?"

Michael doesn't understand what they're saying, but he thinks he hears Mary's name. He heads up the stairs and over to them.

"I think this young man is trying to find her," says the younger woman.

Michael pulls the photo out of his pocket and hands it to the older German woman.

"Yes, I think this is Mary," she says. "Mary Johanson. Maybe many years ago before the war. It's hard to tell. She was burned very badly in the war."

Michael can't make out what she's saying. But he knows the German word for war. "Yes...kreig... the kreig! Can you please tell me where she is? I have a message to give her from the war...you know the kreig!"

The older woman's eyebrows pull together. "The Kreig?"

"I think he wants to know where this Mary is now," says the younger woman. "Something about the war."

"Tell him to wait here." The older woman turns and shuffles back into her apartment. The younger woman doesn't say a word, but instead grabs Michael by the arm to keep him there.

A few seconds later, the older woman returns with a piece of paper. She smiles at Michael and presses the piece of paper into his hand. Michael sees an address and Mary's last name on the paper and smiles back. He puts his hands together and bows to the women. "Danke schoen...danke schoen!" Then he runs down the staircase and out the building's door.

The younger woman looks at the older woman and points to her head. "Crazy Americans!"

Michael jumps into the cab and hands the driver the address. After twenty minutes, they pull up to a nursing home. Michael pays the driver and strides up the steps to the front door. He halts. "Damn," he sighs. "I forgot to get the flowers...oh well."

Inside the nursing home, Michael passes old ladies playing cards on his way to the front desk. The receptionist is Krista Tolle who was Kristin Neavaeh in Michael's previous life. Krista sees Michael standing before her with a strange look on his face.

Michael can't take his eyes off her. She's the most beautiful woman he's ever seen. Krista drums her fingers on the desk waiting.

Finally, Michael gets his book out of his pocket and starts thumbing through the pages.

"A...bitte...I..."

"Yes, may I help you?"

"Ah," says Michael, "you speak American?"

"No, I speak English."

Michael doesn't know what to say next. He is dazed.

"What is it that you want?" asks Krista.

"Boy, that's a loaded question. My name is Michael...Michael Muller. And...uh...I, well, I...was..."

"Are you lost?"

"No, no. Not anymore, thank God."

"Good, let's start at the beginning again alright? You are Michael Muller and you are here...for?"

"Yes...I'm looking for a woman. Her name is Mary, Mary Johanson. I hope she might still be living here."

"Yes, Mary is here."

"Wow...that's great...she's here."

"Are you a friend or family?"

"I guess you would say a friend. Because I'm sure not family."

"That's very nice that you're here to see her."

"Why would you say that?"

"Because as long as I've been here, I can't remember anyone coming to visit Mary."

"How sad."

"It is sad, because she is a very sweet lady. I'll show you to her room. It's just around the corner."

"Perfect."

"Oh, by the way, she speaks English too."

"You mean American?"

"You're a funny guy."

Michael follows Krista about five feet behind so he can get a full look at her walking. He mouths the word "WOW!"

"Oh," says Krista over her shoulder. " I have to tell you she isn't all there in the head, if you know what I mean."

"That's just great."

"What?"

"That's just great that you can show me the way to her room."

"Oh."

"Has she been here a long time?"

"I really don't know. I think awhile. Here it

is." Krista comes to Mary's room and knocks lightly. "Mary, you have a visitor. Michael is here to see you."

Krista hears nothing. She opens the door halfway and peeks in. Krista turns to Michael and smiles. "I think it is alright to go in now. If you should need me for anything, I'll be at the front desk."

"There is one thing you can do for me. Please tell me your name."

"Krista Tolle."

"That is truly beautiful."

Michael holds out his hand to shake hers. Krista shakes his hand. Michael gazes into her eyes and doesn't release her hand right away. Krista, quite irritated, tugs her hand back. "Good bye, Michael!"

Chapter 33

A Message from an Angel

Michael sticks his head into the darkened room. The only light comes from one large window where Mary sits in her wheelchair. She's facing the window and her back is to Michael. "Mary, can I come in?" he asks.

"Michael, is it you?"

"Michael steps closer and when Mary turns to him, he is horrified—her face has been totally disfigured by fire. Michael quickly tries to compose himself. "My name is Michael Muller. I've come a long way to see you."

"Michael? I had a son named Michael too. He died in the war many years ago. Were you in the war too?"

"No. No I wasn't born yet, but my father was in the war."

"Please, feel free to sit down Michael. I've been waiting for you."

Michael pulls up a chair and sits next to Mary. She'd been waiting for him? He wonders. Well, Kristin said Mary wasn't all there in the head.

"It's a good thing you weren't in the war," says Mary, "or any war for that matter. I lost everyone in the war. All the people I ever loved, my parents, my daughter, my husband, and my son, Michael."

"Yes, I know," says Michael.

"How would you know this?"

"Um...well, my father knew your son in the war."

"Really? Did they fight together? What is your father's name?"

"Um...yeah...I guess you could say they fought together. My father's name is James...James Muller."

Mary scratches at the scars on her cheek. "James? I knew all my son's friends in the war and he never mentioned a James."

"Well, you see—"

"And what kind of German name is James anyway?" Mary's voice rises in agitation. "You are lying to me. You're an American, not a German. What are you doing here? What do you want from me?"

"Please...I must tell you—"

"Leave right now. I don't want to hear anything you have to say. Why would you come to torment some poor old woman?"

When Mary starts to push her wheelchair away from Michael, he stands up, pleading. "My father did know your son. You must believe me." He pulls the photo out of his pocket and hands it to Mary.

Mary's eyes widen and her jaw drops open. "This is the photo I sent to Michael, when he was in the war. I put my new address on the back, after the fire. Where did you get this?"

"Your son gave it to my father when he was dying. They were... um...together."

"Oh my God," murmurs Mary, her eyes brimming with tears. "I don't believe it. After all these years." She wipes the tears from her eyes. "So where is your father now?"

Michael doesn't know what to say. "Uh...he's dead. Yep, very dead."

"That's too bad. I would have liked to have talked to him."

Michael sits back down needing to change the subject. "Would you by any chance have a picture of your son?"

"Why, yes of course."

Mary wheels herself over to the dresser and retrieves a shoebox. Then she returns to Michael with a photo. The minute Michael sees it, he gets chills and goose bumps. "God, I must be getting sick."

"Why do you say that?"

"Ever since I got to Germany, I've been getting these chills and these kind of...like goose bumps."

"My grandmother used to say that when you get goose bumps, you need to remember something really important."

"Huh," says Michael. "I don't seem to have anything important to remember."

Mary shows him another photo from the shoebox. "Here is my Eric and Leni. It's the only picture I have of Eric smiling with Leni. Eric never really liked her."

"Why not?"

"I never told anyone this before. But since everyone is dead, what difference does it make now? In 1922, I had an affair with a Jewish man. He was a widower. We were both very lonely. Eric was working out of the country at the time. Leni was born nine months later. Since Eric and I were both good Catholics, we didn't divorce. However Eric and his family never did forgive me—or Leni. So, my poor Leni never received a father's love, from Eric or her real father Kort Nevaeh. What made things even worse is Michael fell in love with Kort's daughter, Kristin. Eric went crazy when he found out."

"Wow...what a story."

"It is, isn't it? And everyone loves a good story, right Michael?"

"Yeah, I guess so. Did you ever tell Michael about his half-sister?"

"No. I was afraid of the shame. But in the end, what was left of our family was destroyed, almost overnight. Eric blamed me for the whole thing. I hated Eric for what he did to Kort, Kristin, and Leni. I know now that the truth we hold back is just as bad as any lie we tell."

"What did he do to Kort and Kristin?"

"Eric killed them both by having his brother Gunther ship them off to a death camp. You see, there was no real love or forgiveness in our family. And in the end we all paid the price. Everyone is dead now but me...and I have been waiting here."

"Waiting for what?"

"I don't really know. Maybe to tell my story to someone. How odd after all these years, it would be to someone like you, a total stranger."

"What's strange is that I had a dream about you," says Michael. "You said something to me about flowers or wait a minute, I think it was roses."

"I had a dream about flowers last night too," says Mary. "Someone brought me yellow roses. I couldn't see his face. But he looked like an angel. I knew that if I could give this person...this angel a message, somehow he could get the message to my son, Michael."

"What was your message?"

"I wanted to tell him four things. First—we are on this planet for only two reasons: to love and forgive each other. Second—always follow your heart and especially your hunches in life. Do you know what I mean when I say this? You know, like those goose bumps you get."

Michael nods. "I think so."

"Third—never follow the heart of any man, country, or religion that believes hate and war are the answers to anything."

"I sure agree with that one."

"Fourth—give your friends and family the best kind of love there is: unconditional love."

"Why not give this kind of love to everyone? Even our enemies."

"Ah, yes. If just a few more people could move out of the illusion of separation—friends versus enemies—and into love, the whole world would change overnight!"

They sit in silence for a moment. Then Michael stands and slowly lifts Mary's frail body out of the wheelchair. With tears in their eyes, they embrace.

"I wish you were my mother," says Michael.

"I'm everyone's mother...and you Michael, are everyone's son."

Michael lowers Mary back down in the wheelchair. She gazes out the window again. "Thank you for coming and visiting me today. Who knows? Maybe you were the one the dream was about."

"When I first saw you today," says Michael, "why did you say you were waiting for me?"

"Are we not all waiting for someone, or something, to change our lives? Are you ready for your life to change, Michael?"

"Yes, I guess I am."

"Then it will!" Mary lets out a sigh. "I'm very tired now."

"It's been a very special time with you," says Michael. "I'll leave you my phone number in America right here on your table, feel free to call me anytime. Aufwiedersehn."

"Aufwiedersehn meine liebe," she whispers.

As Michael walks towards the door, he sees a photo on the wall of Mary, Eric, Leni, and Michael. Below the photo is a bookcase stacked with books. One of the titles is "The Persistent Illusion." Michael puts the paper with his phone number on a small table.

Chapter 34

Love at First Sight?

When Michael reaches the front desk, he finds Krista there reading a book. "How did your visit with Mary go?" she asks, not looking up from the pages.

"Weird. Amazing. Life changing."

"Oh...really?"

"Yes, really Krista. Just like you knowing me will be life changing too!"

Krista peers up from her book. "Really?"

"Yes...really!"

"Then, I guess the real question is: will that change be for better, or for worse?"

"I guess we'll just have to find out, won't we?"

Krista smiles. She hasn't met anyone this cocky in a long time. "You think so, huh?"

"Yep. I think so. I think we should get together tonight over dinner and talk about our life together."

Krista's smile fades and her voice becomes stiff. "I'm afraid that's not possible."

"And why not?"

"For starters, I'm engaged to be married. And even if I wasn't engaged, I'm not attracted to smart-ass American guys."

Michael stands there crushed. "Well...uh...I..."

"Well...what Michael?"

Michael grabs a piece of paper and pen and writes down a phone number on it. Then he hands it to Krista. "Call me if you change your mind."

"Change my mind? Change my mind about what?"

"Uh...I guess...about your boyfriend."

"Good bye, Michael."

As Michael heads out, he calls over his shoulder. "You really need to call me sometime Krista. I'm telling you, he's not the guy for you."

"Good bye, Michael!" yells Krista. She throws Michael's phone number in the trashcan.

Michael walks out of the nursing home and stops on the steps. He looks around at people strolling by on the street and shakes his head. So much for love at first sight! He thinks.

Chapter 35

Beer, Nazis, and Women

The sun is beginning to set on another beautiful September day. The biggest party in the world is in full swing. People from all over the world have come to enjoy Munich's Oktoberfest. Michael and Kirk sit outside under a huge white tent at one of the largest beer gardens in Munich, the Houfbrau house. They're among thousands of people, all drinking beer, laughing, and singing.

Many empty steins sit on Michael and Kirk's table.

"Then...Mary treated me like a son...can you believe that?" asks Michael, slurring his words.

"Yeah, yeah...great," says Kirk who is as drunk as Michael, "but tell me about the hot babe again... what's her name?"

Michael holds up both hands and cups them to his chest about the same place a woman's breasts would be. "Krista...she had the biggest... and the most amazing...eyes!"

Kirk laughs. "Michael...Michael. Do you know what you are? You're a big jerk."

"Yep...you're so right. What was I thinking? I'm just a big jerk. But...Kirk do you believe in love at first sight? Because I think—"

"No. But I believe in lust at first sight. I propose a toast to you Michael, the biggest jerk on the planet."

Kirk and Michael clink their beer glasses and drink. Then Michael folds his arms on the table and rests his head.

Erika Tolle, Krista Tolle's identical twin sister, sets two beer steins down in front of Michael and Kirk. She's dressed in the traditional festive dress with a yellow rose in her hair. "So, boys, have we had too much beer for one day?" She asks in broken English.

When Michael raises his head to see who is speaking, his eyes bulge out. "Oh my God! How could this be?"

"What?" asks Erica. "How could you have too much beer? It's simple. You buy beer...you drink beer... then you drink too much beer."

"No...no... It's you! Kirk this is her...this is..." Michael stands up and tries to take a step towards Erica. He sways to one side, bumping into a young German skinhead. The skinhead's beer spills out all over his black leather jacket and onto his two skinhead friends.

"Hey, I'm really sorry guys," stammers Michael, "but I have to talk to...Kr..."

Michael sees the large swastika tattooed on the skinhead's fist right before it hits him in the face. He slams to the ground. Ericka spins away and into the crowd.

Kirk jumps up and taps the skinhead on the shoulder. "Hey, Nazi dude! We didn't take any of your shit in the war and we're not taking any of it now!"

The skinhead turns to look at Kirk.

"Seig Heil!" says Kirk as he punches him in

the mouth. The skinhead is none other then Frank Costello. Frank's friends jump onto Kirk's back. Michael leaps up. It's a big brawl.

Hours later, Michael and Kirk get out of a police car in front of Kirk's aunt's house. They both look pretty beat up. The police officer sticks his head out of the car window. "My friends," he says, "the war is over and has been for a long time. We Germans are not proud of what happened in this country many years ago. Just like someday your government will not be so proud of what it's doing in Vietnam and other places around the world. I wish somehow you were both Germans...then you might know what I'm talking about. Please don't go back to the Houfbrau House. You are no longer welcome there. Aufwiedersehen."

Michael is too tired and hung over to say anything. Kirk doesn't reply either.

As soon as they're inside the house, Kirk heads up the stairs. "I'm hitting the sack."

Michael goes into the kitchen and to get some ice for his face. He finds Lenny eating a sandwich at the table. "What happened to you guys?" asks Lenny.

"Beer, Nazis, and women."

"Hmmm... Okay... I'm afraid I have some bad news, Michael."

"Great, now what?"

"I got a call from Dad today.... He said you got a letter and—"

"And what?"

"You've been drafted," says Lenny.

"No fucking way!"

The phone rings. "Now what?" Michael growls. He picks up the phone. "Yeah... what do you want?"

"I'm looking for Michael Muller."

"Yes...this is Michael Muller. Krista is that you?"

"Michael?"

"Yes! How are you doing?"

"Not so good... I..." Michael grins. This is the call he's been waiting for. "That's nice."

"What?" Krista sounds confused.

"No! I mean.... It's nice you're calling me."

"I have some bad news. Mary Johanson died... and—"

"Oh no. When?"

"The same day you saw her. I think you may have been the last person to see her alive. Anyway her funeral will be tomorrow and I thought you might like to attend the service."

"That was three days ago. Why didn't you call me sooner?"

"Well... I threw your phone number away. We were going through Mary's things. We found your American phone number in her room today. I called your home in California and talked to your mother. She gave us your number here in Germany. So there we are."

"I still can't believe it." Michael finds a piece of paper and a pencil on the kitchen table and absently starts doodling. The first thing he draws is a casket.

"Can you come to the funeral service tomorrow?" asks Krista.

"Yes, of course. Where is it?"

"Ostfriedhof Cemetery. 6:00 p.m. The Johanson family plot is on the southwest end of the cemetery. Just look for a large stone angel pointing skyward."

Michael doodles an angel and the ass end of a mule on the piece of paper. "Thank you for all your help," he says. "I'm afraid I have been kind of an ass to you. And today...at the Haufbrau House when—"

"Yes...you have been. I would like you to meet my fiancé and sister. I've told them about you and how nice you were to visit Mary. My sister Ericka likes... how do you say? American smart asses."

Michael doodles three stick figures: two girls and one boy. He draws a big X through the boy's figure. "That's just great," he says sarcastically. "I get to meet your sister and your fiancé too. I can't wait to meet them both. I'm sure she's really nice." He draws a bunch of dots on the second girl's face.

"I really need to go, Michael. It's late. We'll see you tomorrow?"

"Yes, of course. Good bye, my friend."

Michael hangs up the phone and studies all his doodles. He draws a large heart with an arrow through it. Then he draws a jagged line going through the heart and a question mark next to it.

Chapter 36

Welcome to My Dream

Michael carries a dozen yellow roses as he walks with Kirk and Lenny through the cemetery. At Mary's gravesite, Michael places the roses on the lid of her coffin. When he looks up, he sees a stone statue of a young angel smiling at him.

The Catholic priest is just finishing up his service. Three old ladies stand next to the coffin. Michael, Kirk, and Lenny join Krista and a young man who are several feet away.

"I'm sorry for being late," Michael whispers to Krista. "I'm afraid we got a little lost."

"It's okay. My sister is late too."

The old ladies glare at Michael and Krista for speaking during the service.

The Catholic priest frowns too and then continues. "In the name of the Father, the Son, and the Holy Spirit. May God have mercy on her soul... Amen." He makes the sign of the cross, as do all the old ladies. Then the priest and ladies walk away.

Krista turns to Michael, Kirk, and Lenny. "This is Hans, my fiancé."

Michael feels a strange shiver as he takes Hans's hand. Hans is Johan Voss, Michael's World War II friend in his past life.

Shaking off the strange feeling, Michael begins his introductions. "This is my brother, Lenny, and my best friend, Kirk. This is Krista, the

girl I was telling you guys about, and...this is her...
uh...boyfriend."

Everyone nods at each other.

"It's weird," says Michael. "Here we are five
total strangers at a gravesite of a woman I hardly
knew."

Krista picks up a medium-sized wooden box off
the ground and hands it to Michael. "We found a note
from Mary. She wanted you to have this."

Michael slowly opens the box. It's full of photos
and a small ring box with Mary's wedding ring.

"Wow," says Lenny. "Why'd she leave all this to
you?"

"I don't know," says Michael.

"Look, there's a note," says Kirk.

"I can't read it," says Michael, "it's in German."

"I'll read it for you," says Krista as she takes the
note from Michael. "Mary writes, 'Michael, I know
this must feel very strange to you. I really couldn't
think of anyone but you to give these things to. It's
funny how sometimes in life you can feel closer
to someone you have only known for just a few
minutes than to people you have known for many
years. That's how I feel about you, my friend.'"
Kristin swallows, then continues. "It's signed Mary...
and there is a P.S. 'Thank you for the roses!'"

Michael rubs his forehead in disbelief. "This
is all so strange," he says. "How did she know about
the flowers?"

"Who knows?" says Krista. "Many people at
the rest home thought she was crazy. She kept talking
about her dead son. How he would come back to her

one day...before she died and that he would bring her flowers."

Kirk pipes in. "Yeah...it seems the older people get, the nuttier they are."

Michael can't take his eyes off a young woman striding over. She looks just like Krista.

"Well, she finally made it!" says Krista.

"Michael," says Krista, "this is my crazy sister Ericka."

Ericka smiles at Michael.

"Ericka," continues Krista, "this is Michael, Kirk, and Lenny."

"I kind of met the boys yesterday at the Haufbrau House. They were trying to start World War III."

"Uh...we...," stammers Kirk.

"That's alright," says Ericka. "Boys will be boys. I'm so sorry I missed the service. I had to work late."

Michael has a silly grin on his face. "I'm just glad you made it."

"Are you now?" Ericka brushes the hair out of her eyes. "Well, we'll just see about that. You haven't got to know me yet. Besides, I hate funerals. They make me so thirsty. So who wants to buy me a drink?"

"Great idea," says Lenny.

"Yeah...let's go," says Kirk.

Ericka walks over to Mary's coffin and takes two of the yellow roses. She gives one of the roses to Krista. Michael and the others give her disapproving looks.

"Hey, she won't miss them," Ericka says sheepishly.

"That's my crazy sister," says Krista.

It's the end of the day, and the sky is streaked with orange and yellow. They all head out of the cemetery and into an adjacent park. It is the same park where Michael and Kristin used to meet in his past life. Lenny and Kirk walk together, followed by Krista and Hans.

Ericka hooks her arm into Michael's as they walk behind everyone else. She holds the rose in her other hand. The stem is so long, the rose drags on the ground.

"So Michael, are you ready for your life to change?" asks Ericka.

"Huh?"

"I'm just kidding. But really, tell me about your political views and how you feel about the war in Vietnam. Are you willing to fight for your country?"

"Oh brother! I guess my mother was right. Things are way more complicated than we'll ever know."

"What are you talking about, Michael?"

"I guess life is one big crazy dream. So welcome to my dream, Erica."

"Really, Michael?" Ericka takes two steps ahead of Michael and throws her rose up over her head and backwards. As she does this, her sleeve falls down her arm. Michael blinks at a tattoo on her forearm. It's of a rose winding around a dagger in the shape of a large letter E.

She glances over her shoulder and says with a glint in her eye, "No Michael, welcome to MY dream!"

The yellow rose flies up into the sunset, then falls to the ground.

Back in the graveyard, the stone angel points skyward with a smile.

The End?

There is no *End*.

Escape from the Persistent Illusion

There is a lot of talk nowadays about "consciousness." "That person is conscious." "We need to be more conscious." "I want to be fully conscious." They say conscious is the quality or state of awareness, of being aware of an external object or something within oneself.

If Albert Einstein was right, then maybe being fully conscious is not all that difficult? Maybe all you have to do, in order to be a fully conscious being, is to wake up from your dream, the illusion of your life. Once you realize you are not your story, then you can no longer be the victim of your story. Yes, enjoy your story, stay on the stage of life, but realize it is just a stage. When the story loses its power over you, you are there, you have made it. The drama is over, the insanity is over, and you have become the Zen master. You are the Buddha! You are a fully conscious entity!

My friend, Jerry Preator, in Portland, Oregon said it perfectly. He said, "Have one foot in this reality and one foot in the next." You will definitely have problems if you are spending too much time in one place or the other.

Waking up from the dream, the illusion, can be a simple thing to say, yet hard to execute at all times. One of the reasons is that we are wired into mammal's bodies. We are programed for fight or flight. It's truly in our DNA. So we are all pre-programed for going into fear. It's pretty much a knee jerk reaction to things coming at us. When the light turns red we slam on the brakes. We usually are not thinking about the illusion of this reality at that moment. Many fears come at us much slower. Sometimes its starts with a simple thought. Our brain takes an idea and starts processing it. The brain enjoys creating different scenarios on how badly things could turn out. What started out as a passing idea is now a major concern. The brain has created the story of a probable outcome. The story looks and feels real. From there we move into the fear.

You can't stop ideas coming into your mind. However when the idea turns into fear, don't let it take control of you. It's easy to go into fear, we all do it. The key is not living there. Pull your energy back. Don't give it power. In fact, take the power from it. It seems the only difference between an ascended master and everyone else is how quickly they can pull their energy back when the illusion looks threatening. The ascended master can recall his energy immediately. The rest of us not so quickly. In fact some people never do.

Some people move into the fear and live there. They have completely identified with form. They love what fear does for them. It's their drug of choice. They love the drama and the insanity of it. They not only like watching the soap operas on TV, they want to live in one too. They are trapped in hell and want you to join them there.

If a person becomes conscious and their partner isn't. Your days together are numbered.

They will not appreciate your unwillingness to getting involved in the drama. The unconscious one will hate your Zen outlook to everything. You will want to help them but it is like trying to describe the color blue to a blind man. They may have a difficult time understanding it.

Here is an interesting question: "If a person has come to this planet to play the story of Hamlet, do you have the right or the obligation to pull him off his stage?" Maybe the answer isn't "yes" or "no." Maybe the answer is, we need to just get out of their way! You can choose to stop your story anytime, but others must make their own decisions concerning their stories.

There is only one person you can change on this planet, and that person will always be yourself.

You have incarnated here not to figure out your parents, your children, your friends, and your lovers. The person you came to figure out is...You! You are the big mystery. Your life is like a giant jigsaw puzzle. Your job is to wake up every day with the idea that someone today will be handing you a piece of your puzzle. They will be giving you a clue of who you really are. Your job is to identify the puzzle piece and add it to the rest of your puzzle. Some of the puzzle pieces you collect are not attractive ones. In fact they can be quite ugly. But they are all part of who you are and your current story. You have come here to be a detective in the greatest story there is. The story of you!

Like any good video game the most difficult ones are the most fun to play. In the video game we are now in called "Planet Earth: The Age of Fear," most people will want to play all the different characters: the heroes, the villains, the monks, the victims, and even the crazies. Just like the video games people play while sitting in front of their televisions, the game "Planet Earth: The Age of Fear" will give you choices. You can choose an "easy" setting in which you can get through all the levels in no time at all, a "medium" setting which is more difficult, and of the course the "hardest" setting. This setting is almost impossible to get through. Of all the different settings on the game, easy, medium, or hard, which one do you feel the most exhilarated getting through? Yes, the hard one. Now look at your life. Which setting did you chose for yourself in your game of life?

We are here to enjoy our lives and to have fun with our stories. Are you enjoying your story? If not, then why not? Have you chosen a tough story, a hard story, or a painful story? Then just remember who you really are. You are a powerful spiritual being having a physical experience. Know on some level, your soul wanted to have this experience. Are you shaking your fist at God and blaming him for your life? Why would your soul have chosen this insane story that you are in now? Ask yourself, what you are supposed to learn from this life lesson? Is it patience, forgiveness, empathy, generosity, or love?

Karma is strange stuff. I have a different spin on Karma. I believe you don't have to come back and marry Bob again. You don't have to come back and "make it right" this time. You don't have to "do" anything. If you want to do something, then wonderful. If you feel you need to have a certain experience, go for it. No one is forcing you to play these roles. Every decision on the other side is done out of love. We have challenged each other to play our different roles. Our guides and friends are helping us out. They are doing this out of love, not fear.

Whatever experiences a soul has created for others, it will eventually want to experience it for itself. Just like any good cook, you will always want to taste what you have created. If the soul has created a living hell for others, it will eventually want to experience it for itself. The soul wants to experience everything, to taste everything, to be everything.

We make agreements or contracts with other entities. We have the most Karma and strongest agreements with parents and children. We pick them before we come here. You can get rid of friends, lovers, and spouses. They come and go. But parents and children will always be with you until you or they die. Everything in your life is not fated. There is a huge percentage of free will mixed into the equation.

Just like in a video game, you can move around quite a bit within the parameters of the game. However, sometimes it will not feel that way. In the Vedic tradition there are times of Rahu. Times of intense karmic activity. Normally there might be 90% free will and 10% Karma going on in your life. However when you are in a Rahu period of your life it will feel more like 90% Karma and only 10% free will going on. Your agreement has kicked in and you are heading towards it, whether you want to or not.

The biggest wild card in the universe is love. Love can change all Karma. The golden rule says it all. To love others, as we love ourselves.

I believe we are perfect. I believe our stories are perfect. There is no fall from grace. There is no "getting it wrong" and there is certainly no going back to "get it right" this time.

There is certainly no God making you pay for your sins. That is the God that churches have created. They have created a God in "their image" instead of the other way around. Their Gods are hateful, vengeful, and jealous and would have no problem sending someone to a burning hell for an eternity. Interesting, few people could put their own child's hand over an open flame, for even a minute. Yet they have no problem believing in a God who would do the same thing to his children in a burning hell for an eternity. The God they worship seems to have less compassion than they do.

Just like in Hollywood, sometimes an actor will choose to play the hero, other times the villain. It really doesn't matter what role he plays because the role he is playing isn't truly him. Just like the roles we are playing in this video game our not truly us.

That is why judgement is never a good thing. What are you judging, the actor, or the role he has chosen? Do you really know this actor on a soul level? We can't judge actors for taking on roles that are beyond their range. So on what bases could we judge anyone and their story?

There is no judgement with God. This is a concept that many people have a problem with. They want their God to judge them and others. The reason is, they judge themselves and others every day. Their lives are full of judgement. The "us and them" illusion and the "good and bad" illusion. Of course with the concept of judgement goes the concept of punishment. With no judgement there can be no punishment.

Whoa! Some people have said. If nothing really matters and there is no judgement and thus no punishment, then I can go out and do anything I want. If it's not real, then what difference does it make?

Yes and no. Yes, it's not real. Yes, you can do whatever you want. However, unconscious people believe that nothing matters except their own story and themselves. They have little or no thought for others. Conscious ones know that everything matters. That whatever they are cooking up for other people could be a meal they may be compelled to experience later for themselves. There are real opportunities here in this game to help others and ourselves, anything else is a waste of spirit.

As you are being taught your life lessons remember that as people are testing you, you are testing other people. We are all teachers. We are all students.

No matter what your story is. No matter who you think you are. No matter who you think the people are in your story—your story will end one day. Every story will end one day.

There is no way out of it. Every day on this planet is getting you one day closer to the big party in the sky. I believe we are going to be as shocked as hell when we make the transition from this world to the next. When we find out how we took the whole thing way too seriously. How we lived our lives in fear and worry and could have lived in ease and grace.

I will be the first to admit it, when that day comes. I know, I'll look around the room in total surprise and say. "Wow...what a jerk I turned out to be!"

I'll see you there.

How I Came to Write this Book

How did this book come about? Good question! I wish I knew. I wish could take credit for the information in it. In truth, I have to tell you this information came from some place other than myself. The book started out as a screen play. Two thirds of the screen play was written in just two weeks. There were times I was typing and had no idea what to write next; I found myself typing things I never thought of. So I truly think of myself as some kind of scribe taking dictation from some higher source.

There are pieces of me in the story. I do believe in reincarnation, even though I was raised in a strict fundamentalist Christian faith—a faith that didn't believe in the concept of reincarnation and the immortality of the soul.

As a small child, like Michael in the story, I too had a strange fascination with the Second World War. For me, I loved to build model German airplanes from the war. I didn't care for the English, American, Russian, or Japanese planes, only German. I loved to watch war movies. I also remember feeling bad for the Germans in the movies because they were usually portrayed as people that were no more than animals. I thought to myself, "There were some good Germans too." My friends and I would play World War II board games for hours on end. In fact up to ten years ago, I thought about the war every day. Yes, it was definitely more than a causal interest. It was a strange kind of obsession.

All this was very strange because I was raised a strict pacifist. As a Jehovah's Witness, I believed in strict neutrality. I was hated in high school because of my stand against the Viet Nam War. I've been spit on and slapped in the face because I would not salute the American flag. My classmates would ask me, "What if everyone felt the way you did and did not go to war?" To which, I would say, "I guess there would be no more war!" My feeling was that God was not partial and I couldn't imagine Jesus saluting one flag over another, if he were on Earth. I guess some of my classmates felt differently. It's truly funny that on this planet, the acceptable behavior is to agree with war and killing. The crazies and weird ones only want peace.

I joined the ministry and moved to Salina Kansas in 1968. I was a conscientious objector during the Viet Nam War and had a 4-D minister classification. From there I went to the headquarters of the Jehovah's Witnesses and worked in their factory for four years. They paid us twenty-two dollars a month, plus room and board. I was a total self-righteous religious zealot by the time I got there.

In 1974, I left the headquarters and got married. I was no longer the religious zealot—just a family man with two kids. It was time to pass the thought system down to them. So every Saturday we would go door to door teaching them how to sell our religious ideas to other people.

In 1987, I went to my twentieth class reunion. Something a good Jehovah's Witness wouldn't do, but I did anyway. I called one of my classmates who was raised as Jehovah's Witness too. He had left the faith in high school and joined the army and went to Viet Nam. I wanted to see him, so I called him up, to invite him to the reunion. He was surprised to hear from me. In the course of conversation, he said, "You know, I went to Viet Nam and I don't have any regrets!" To which I said, "Well, I didn't go to Viet Nam and I have no regrets either."

I found out at the reunion that at least five of my classmates had come back from the war and took their own lives. So at least a couple of my classmates had some regrets about the war.

Something interesting happened at the reunion. During the party, one of my classmates came up to me and said, "I really need to talk to you when you have a minute." I was a little nervous about talking to him. As I mentioned I had few friends and was not liked in high school because of my antiwar stance. Even though we had known each other for many years since elementary school, I had no idea why he would want to talk to me in private. I got up from the table and went to the lobby where he was standing. He had a strange look on his face. I really didn't know if I was going to get a slap or a hug from him. He said, "You Know Keith, I went to Viet Nam. I thought a lot about you over there." Here it comes I thought. "I thought about you when we were both in elementary school together. How we would all be standing there saluting the flag every morning and you would just stand there with your arms by your side saying nothing. I just wanted to tell you, I really respect you for that."

There are many things I appreciate about how I was raised as a Jehovah's Witness, besides their neutrality in all political matters. Yet in 2001, I left that thought system too. The reason is they too had the "us and them" mind set. They were right and all other religions were wrong. When I left their faith, I paid the full price. I left the "us" of being a Jehovah's Witness and became one of the "them"—a nonbeliever. Because shunning is a part of their believe system, I lost almost everything: all my friends, a sister of fifty years, a wife of twenty-seven years and most of my business. I was shunned and haven't been able to talk to these people in over fifteen years. It was so bad that when my father died in 2012, my sister wouldn't even call to let me know he had passed. It was "our way or the highway" and I was on the highway.

It's all perfect. I know on a spirit level, I set this story up on the other side. So no sour grapes here. It's my story and I helped to create it, on a soul level.

In fact, one psychic reading put many of the pieces of the puzzle together for me. After I left the witnesses, I had a psychic reading. The first question I had for her was about the war. "I think about the war all the time, why is that?"

She said, "You were a solider in the war and died in it."

I thought that made perfect sense. I asked, "What nationality was I?"

She said, "I see a gray uniform...you were a German."

That made sense too. So I asked, "What branch of service was I in?"

She said, "You were a pilot!"

Since I liked to build model German planes as a kid, that added another piece of the puzzle. Then she told me something that I had no idea about. She said, "You didn't like what the Germans were doing in the war and you killed yourself." She went on to say, "You come from a predominately Nazi family and you didn't have the courage to stand up to them. So you took your own life."

Wow, my lifetime as a Jehovah's Witnesses made sense now. When I was born in 1949, the Nazis were all gone but there was a great Nazi-like religion I could be put into. *Your job, (like the mission impossible quote) if you choose to accept, will be to stand up to them and make a stand against the "us and them" mind set.* What could be more perfect? That was exactly what I did. I was very vocal about my exit and leaving that faith. I was even on the front page of *The Oregonian* on March 22, 2002. I feel I stood up and did what I should have done back in the war. They say that those who commit suicide usually come back quicker than those experiencing other kinds of deaths, to face whatever obstacles they couldn't get through. Since that first psychic visit, I've had many past life regressions and channelings all confirming my World War II lifetime.

I'm not here to judge people and their Karma. I know I've been a warrior many lifetimes. I know on a soul level, I've killed and died for my belief systems many times. What's changed about me? I'm just not proud of it anymore. Is there anything to be proud about when it comes to war and killing? This "us and them" that I have been a part of, and the rest of the planet is enjoying so much of, is tearing us apart. I hope it will be different one day.

There are other true events that happen in the book. My father was the soldier who got his face slapped by my mother on the dance floor, for putting his hands in the wrong place. Soldiers did die by drinking poison that they thought was wine. Believe it or not, I talked to a woman whose husband was an interpreter during the war. After he shot a German soldier, he did talk to him for a few minutes before he died. The dying man handed a photo of his wife and two blond little girls to the man who had taken his life. He requested he contact his family after the war.

Other things in the book, like love at first sight, have happened to me. Love at first sight is really recognition at first sight. Having an instant like or dislike of people on the spot are all things I've experienced. All the things we know in our soul that there is no explanation for.

As for déjà vu, even my father, who was like Archie Bunker and didn't believe in anything, even thought twice about it. He told me how he had gone to El Salvador with his wife. They were visiting a remote town where she grew up—a place he had never been before and certainly never saw before. He told me how he knew the city like the back of his hand. He told me that he knew where a church would be even before he saw it. He said, "How could I know such a thing?" I said, "You must have been there before." He said, "No, I was never there before." I said, "No, Dad you must have been there before." To which he said, "Oh that bull shit!" I've heard of countless stories of people visiting places they feel a strange connection to.

I drove a taxi in Portland Oregon for six months in 2008, it was one of the most spiritual things I've ever done. I drove people to get chemotherapy. I drove strippers and prostitutes to work. I set there listening to people's stories. We laughed and cried together. I found out that everyone has a story. Most the people in my cab totally believed their story was real!

So yes, we do make our own living hells by believing our stories are real.

One of the movies that changed my life was Bill Murray's *The Razor's Edge*. A friend of mine bought Somerset Maugham's book of the same title and gave it to me. It was amazing. It was written in the 1920s and was nothing like the movie. However, it truly opened me up to other thought systems and the concept of reincarnation.

When the student is ready the teacher arrives.

I hope this information in this book has given you a sense of greater peace.

On the other hand, if you feel no connection to this information, that's fine too.

As a Jehovah's Witness, I spent thousands of hours knocking on doors trying to sell our thought system to other people. I'm not trying to sell ideas anymore. The opinions in this book are just that, opinions. Just another possible way of looking at things.

It's funny to look back at ourselves and where we have come from. If me at sixty-five years old met myself at twenty-one years old and we sat down and had a conversation together, if we exchanged ideas about our belief systems and our stories, both of us would think the other were insane. Just like the twenty-year-old Art Garfunkel talking to Marcel Dalio at 107 years old, in the movie *Catch 22*. I feel like I have been both these characters in this life. The stupid kid and the wise old man. The ultimate "us" and "them," you and yourself.

My twenty-one-year-old self would have no problem pouring gas on my sixty-five-year-old self and setting me on fire. So really, how can we take what we currently think so seriously? It's just going to change next year, or next lifetime.

The only real constancy in life is change and people become the things they hate every day. Just ask Frank Costello.

Life is a journey and everyone's journey should be respected.

So I guess we need to cut ourselves and others some serious slack. There is no "us" and "them" in yourself and there is certainly no "us" and "them" with others. There is only us.

Namasté,

Keith Casarona
newboy499@hotmail.com

Acknowledgments

To Naomi, for breathing life into my screen play.

To Eckhart, Neal, Caroline, Robert, Michael and all the others who have helped us remember who we really are.

To Kelly and Kaisan, my two best friends who stuck beside me when no one else would.

To Sherilyn my old friend who has shared the gift of love again with me in this lifetime.

Made in the USA
Columbia, SC
08 October 2020